THE SORROWS OF YOUNG WERTHER

JOHANN WOLFGANG VON GOETHE was born in 1749, the son of a well-to-do citizen of Frankfurt. As a young man he studied law and briefly practised as a lawyer, but creative writing was his chief concern. In the early 1770s he was the dominating figure of the German literary revival, his tragic novel *Werther* bringing him international fame.

In 1775 he settled permanently in the small duchy of Weimar where he became a minister of state and director of the court theatre; in 1782 he was ennobled as 'von Goethe'. His journey to Italy in 1786–8 influenced the development of his mature classical style; in the 1790s he and his younger contemporary Schiller (1759–1805) were the joint architects of Weimar Classicism, the central phase of German literary culture.

Goethe wrote in all the literary genres but his interests extended far beyond literature and included a number of scientific subjects. His creative energies never ceased to take new forms and he was still writing original poetry at the age of more than eighty. In 1806 he married Christiane Vulpius (1765–1816), having lived with her for eighteen years; they had one surviving son, August (1789–1830). Goethe died in 1832.

DAVID CONSTANTINE is a poet and translator, and co-editor (with Helen Constantine) of the journal *Modern Poetry in Translation*. He has published volumes of poetry, short stories, and a novel, and is a translator of Hölderlin, Goethe, Kleist, and Brecht. His translations of Goethe's *Faust, Parts I* and *II* are published by Penguin, and his translation of *Elective Affinities* is in Oxford World's Classics. In 2010 he won the BBC National Short Story Award.

OXFORD WORLD'S CLASSICS

*For over 100 years Oxford World's Classics have brought
readers closer to the world's great literature. Now with over 700
titles—from the 4,000-year-old myths of Mesopotamia to the
twentieth century's greatest novels—the series makes available
lesser-known as well as celebrated writing.*

*The pocket-sized hardbacks of the early years contained
introductions by Virginia Woolf, T. S. Eliot, Graham Greene,
and other literary figures which enriched the experience of reading.
Today the series is recognized for its fine scholarship and
reliability in texts that span world literature, drama and poetry,
religion, philosophy, and politics. Each edition includes perceptive
commentary and essential background information to meet the
changing needs of readers.*

OXFORD WORLD'S CLASSICS

JOHANN WOLFGANG VON GOETHE

The Sorrows of Young Werther

Translated with an Introduction and Notes by
DAVID CONSTANTINE

OXFORD
UNIVERSITY PRESS

OXFORD
UNIVERSITY PRESS

Great Clarendon Street, Oxford OX2 6DP

Oxford University Press is a department of the University of Oxford.
It furthers the University's objective of excellence in research, scholarship,
and education by publishing worldwide in

Oxford New York

Auckland Cape Town Dar es Salaam Hong Kong Karachi
Kuala Lumpur Madrid Melbourne Mexico City Nairobi
New Delhi Shanghai Taipei Toronto

With offices in

Argentina Austria Brazil Chile Czech Republic France Greece
Guatemala Hungary Italy Japan Poland Portugal Singapore
South Korea Switzerland Thailand Turkey Ukraine Vietnam

Oxford is a registered trade mark of Oxford University Press
in the UK and in certain other countries

Published in the United States
by Oxford University Press Inc., New York

© David Constantine 2012

The moral rights of the author have been asserted
Database right Oxford University Press (maker)

First published as an Oxford World's Classics paperback 2012

All rights reserved. No part of this publication may be reproduced,
stored in a retrieval system, or transmitted, in any form or by any means,
without the prior permission in writing of Oxford University Press,
or as expressly permitted by law, or under terms agreed with the appropriate
reprographics rights organization. Enquiries concerning reproduction
outside the scope of the above should be sent to the Rights Department,
Oxford University Press, at the address above

You must not circulate this book in any other binding or cover
and you must impose this same condition on any acquirer

British Library Cataloguing in Publication Data

Data available

Library of Congress Cataloging in Publication Data

Library of Congress Control Number: 2011939885

Typeset by Cenveo, Bangalore, India
Printed in Great Britain
on acid-free paper by
Clays Ltd, St Ives plc

ISBN 978-0-19-958302-7

3

CONTENTS

INTRODUCTION

Die Leiden des jungen Werthers (*The Sorrows of Young Werther*), published in the autumn of 1774, made Goethe's name; but for three or four years before then he had already been writing with great self-confidence and distinction. Briefly as a young student in Leipzig he adopted the poetic tone and manners of his urbane rococo contemporaries; but moving to Strasbourg in 1770 and meeting the critic and philosopher Herder, he was directed by him into ballads, folk-songs, the deeply congenial world of so-called primitive song. Characteristically, that literary influence conjoined at once with a passionate love—for Friederike Brion—and in poems addressed to her—'Mailied', 'Heidenröslein', 'Willkommen und Abschied'—he broke through into his own poetic voice. With his early work on *Faust* (the so-called *Urfaust*), and the 'Shakespearian' chronicle-play *Götz von Berlichingen* and a dozen more vital and characteristic poems ('Der Wandrer', 'Wandrers Sturmlied', 'Mahometsgesang', 'Ganymed'…), Goethe's achievement by his mid-twenties was prodigious in its originality, force, and variety. *Götz*, written and published in 1773, was first performed in April 1774 in Berlin, and by the end of that year, after *Werther*'s appearance in September, Goethe had become, as Byron said half a century later, 'the first literary character in Europe'.

Goethe was the chief maker of the movement in German literature known as *Sturm und Drang* (literally, 'storm and stress'). There were other gifted and important writers in it too, J. M. R. Lenz, for example, and, at the end of the period, Friedrich Schiller; but Goethe was pre-eminent and, unlike others, moved on, sloughing off one skin for the next (the image is his). *Sturm und Drang* in its language, gestures, forms, was a literature of revolt. Enlisting Shakespeare, the writers sought to uncover a culture of their own from under the dead tradition of the French; to be more natural, more local, achieve an identity. There was a social and political edge to this, most obvious in Goethe's *Urfaust* (not published till 1887), Schiller's *Die Räuber* (*The Robbers*), and Lenz's *Der*

Hofmeister (*The Tutor*), but the successful revolt was all literary, benefiting later writers, among them the politically far more definite Georg Büchner and Bertolt Brecht.

Sturm und Drang is usually studied as a distinct period of German literature, separate from Germany's own Romanticism (Novalis, Tieck, Friedrich Schlegel, Brentano) and those of Britain and France; but really, from a larger perspective, it belongs in the context of a European Romanticism beginning in the 1760s. Viewed like that, Goethe was and, despite his later Classicism, remained, a Romantic writer and *Werther* is a Romantic text. In that novel, in his early *Faust*, and in dozens of lyric poems he was already in the 1770s asserting, as Keats would nearly fifty years later, 'the holiness of the heart's affections' in 'the true voice of feeling'. The relative naturalism of his language anticipates Wordsworth's championing, in the Preface to the *Lyrical Ballads* (1798/1800), of the use in poetry of 'the real language of men'. And most strikingly, what Werther suffers and describes in his letter of 3 November, that loss of spirit, is the anxiety and horror in the heart of all Romanticism that Coleridge called, in his ode of that name (1802), 'dejection'—when the genial spirits fail, when the 'shaping spirit of Imagination' cannot sustain any vital connection between the subject and the world.

The Makings of Werther

Goethe was—he said so himself—a 'confessional' writer; that is, what he wrote came in large measure out of the life he lived. How directly and obviously depended of course on the project in hand— poems, fictions, plays have their own determinants—and, somewhat, on the phase of life in which he wrote. *Werther* (1774) and *Elective Affinities* (1809) are both novels. Of the latter he said, 'I lived every word of [it]'; but also, his chronicler Eckermann reports: 'He said there was nothing in his *Elective Affinities* which had not been really lived, but nothing was there in the form *in which* it had been lived.'[1] But when *Werther* came out the people close to it and

---

[1] J. P. Eckermann, *Gespräche mit Goethe in den letzten Jahren seines Lebens* (1837–48), 9 Feb. 1829 and 17 Feb. 1830.

soon everybody else quite understandably believed that much or even most of it had really been lived *and in that form*.

In part it is a matter of genre. Lyric poems may be very autobiographical and many of Goethe's are, in all the phases of his life; but novels and stories are more likely to induce readers to wonder are the characters and situations 'true' because, if written at all in the realist mode, they need more of the real world's details for their existence and effect than poems do. For *Werther*, his first novel, Goethe used the stuff of his own and other people's lives with a quite extraordinary immediacy and ruthlessness.

There are three main contributions of biographical and autobiographical fact to the making of *Werther*: the triangle: Goethe–Christian Kestner–Charlotte Buff (who became Kestner's wife); the life and suicide of Karl Wilhelm Jerusalem; and the triangle: Goethe–Peter Anton Brentano–Maximiliane von La Roche (who became Brentano's wife).

Goethe moved to Wetzlar in May 1772 to get some practical experience of law, the profession he had studied for and in which he took no interest. There he got to know Christian Kestner, a secretary at the courts, and, at a dance on 9 June, the young woman Kestner intended to marry, Charlotte Buff. In March of the previous year her mother had died, leaving her, then aged eighteen, the second-oldest of twelve children, to look after the family and manage the household. Goethe, Kestner, and Charlotte became a close trio; and to her family also Goethe was fondly attached. In a fashion already characteristic, he broke out of the entanglement and left Wetzlar without warning on 11 September, and on foot and by boat made his way down the Lahn to Koblenz, where he met the sixteen-year-old Maximiliane von La Roche. He was back home in Frankfurt by the nineteenth.

In book 13 of his autobiography *Dichtung und Wahrheit* (*Poetry and Truth*) Goethe had this to say about quitting Charlotte Buff and meeting Maximiliane von La Roche: 'It is a very pleasant feeling when a new passion starts in us before the old has quite lapsed—as at sunset when we see the moon rising opposite and enjoy the double radiance of both heavenly lights.' The fictional Lotte, mostly Charlotte Buff, has Maximiliane's black eyes.

Goethe and Karl Wilhelm Jerusalem had been students together for two years (1765–7) in Leipzig and renewed their aquaintance-ship, never very cordial, in Wetzlar. Jerusalem, an amateur of the arts and philosophy, held a secretarial post; got on badly with his superior, an envoy at the Court; and was in love with a married woman by the name of Elisabeth Herd who didn't love him and complained about him to her husband. Jerusalem shot himself on the night of 29–30 October 1772. Goethe, back in Wetzlar in early November, appalled by this event, found out all he could about it and his chief source was Kestner who wrote, perhaps at Goethe's bidding, an extraordinarily full account, much of which Goethe utilized for *Werther*. During the rest of November 1772 Goethe busied himself collecting details about Jerusalem rather as the Editor in his novel would about the fictional Werther. He put many of these biographical facts as well as many details of his own rela-tionship with Kestner and Charlotte directly into the novel, as though he were indeed the editor and/or narrator of his own ter-minated life. Years later in *Dichtung und Wahrheit* he wrote another version. *Werther*, near the beginning of his career, is a particularly drastic example of the compulsive working and reworking of the stuff of life, his own and other people's, that would be Goethe's way of being in the world for the rest of his days.

Kestner and Charlotte were married on 4 April 1773, but nei-ther that nor Jerusalem's suicide was the immediate catalyst for the writing of *Werther*. Goethe saw the La Roches, mother and daugh-ter, intelligent, artistically gifted and lively women, in Frankfurt that August. When he saw Maximiliane next, in January 1774, again in Frankfurt, she was married—to the businessman Peter Anton Brentano, more than twenty years her senior and a widower with five children whom she had to look after. For those two weeks in January Goethe continued his relationship with her. They were like brother and sister, he recalls in *Dichtung und Wahrheit*, far closer in age than she and her husband, while he was, Goethe says, 'the only one in her entire circle in whom she could hear an echo of that music of the intellect and the spirit to which in girlhood she had grown accustomed'. But Brentano was no Kestner and did not in the least want Goethe in his family. Maximiliane bore Brentano twelve children (among them Bettina and Clemens, two Romantic writers) and died in 1793, aged thirty-seven.

Maximiliane and her mother left Frankfurt 31 January 1774 and Goethe began writing *Werther* next day. He saw that the three chief biographical ingredients listed above could be made into a novel which would fuse and exceed them. He describes the writing thus in book 13 of *Dichtung und Wahrheit*:

I had entirely isolated myself, indeed I had forbidden my friends to visit me. Inwardly also I put to one side everything that did not belong to my project but gathered together everything that had any bearing on it. I went over my recent life, the stuff of which I had not yet put to any poetic use. In those conditions, after long and manifold and secret preparations, I wrote *Werther* in four weeks without beforehand setting down any plan of the whole thing or the treatment of any of its parts.

Writing, he understood the figurative life of the characters and circumstances he was so precisely shaping: how they could stand for the society he lived in and were, furthermore (which is why the novel lasts) archetypal in their pattern and their fate.

The project magnetizes certain real details, those it can use, draws them along with it in a shaping process, leaves aside those, perhaps important in 'the real story', in which it has no interest, and invents others which were not in that story at all. The project is a novel, it derives from and bears powerfully upon real life but it is a work of fiction, making its own truth as it goes along, taking, shaping, discarding always and only in the interest of—to get closer and more finely to—that truth. It is this mixture of apparent fidelity to some of the facts and apparent indifference to or recklessness with others that people involved in the lived story found so disconcerting when they read the novel that came out of it. Hence Kestner's touching complaint that 'his' Lotte would never have been so forward as to organize a counting game and slap the players when they made a mistake. And quite understandably he did not like the portrayal of himself as Albert. But for the writer all that matters is the truth of the novel, of the fiction he is making; which truth stands in a complex and vital relationship with the factual truth but is not it, is not seeking to be it, seeks only its own. All writers who draw on the lives they live among other people act and must act like this—D. H. Lawrence's friends were often appalled and hurt by what he had 'done to them' in his fictions—and Goethe in *Werther*, his first novel, was already astonishingly aware of his duty, as a writer, to the truth of fiction, and of the fraught and unstable relationship there will always be between a novel and the lived life it springs from. By employing an Editor—a scrupulous collector of the material—Goethe, in a way common among novelists then, ostensibly authenticates his account and encourages readers to feel that these things really happened. At the same time (more of this later), he allows the Editor to exceed his role and to become, in effect, an omniscient narrator; which is to say, to become quite blatantly what he was anyway: an agent of fiction.

And what is the truth even of the 'real' story? The Editor reports that whilst he found general agreement as to the facts, there were differing views as to the ways of thinking and feeling ('Sinnesarten') of the people involved. He diligently collects and presents every scrap of documentary evidence, because, he says, 'it is so difficult to uncover the very particular true motivations of even one action when it occurs among people who are not of the common run'. Even the documents themselves are, of course, by no means unequivocal. The truth is, we live among fictions. All our thinking, feeling, and writing makes up versions of what we like to call reality; and our versions are subject to continual alteration with the passage of time and under the impress of other people's versions. Novels and poems, which are fictions made of the stuff of life, again and again will alter our decided versions of the lives we have lived and are living now. Beyond any doubt, Goethe's *Werther* altered the way its readers viewed their lives; doubtless many lived or wished to live differently because of it. And that effect is latent in the novel still. Any reader may activate it.

The Form of Werther

The story of *Werther* (or most of it) is told in letters. The epistolary novel was well established in European fiction by the time

Goethe came to use it. Jean-Jacques Rousseau and Samuel Richardson before him, Choderlos de Laclos after him, are masters of the form; and comparing *Werther* with their great novels— Richardson's *Pamela* (1740–1) and *Clarissa* (1748–9), Rousseau's *Julie, ou La Nouvelle Éloise* (1761), and Laclos's *Les Liaisons dangereuses* (1782)—at once reveals its peculiarity. A story told in letters, presented as real documents, pleases readers who like to think it really happened. Goethe will have chosen the form for its immediacy, its inherent sense of life being lived. Werther writes his letters very soon after the lived events. Or he breaks off a letter to go on with the life he is describing in it. And he writes his last up to the very moment of his death. All these are possibilities inherent in the chosen form. But there is another—a large and abundant resource—which Goethe chooses not to employ. The novels of Richardson and Laclos revel in a multiplicity of perspectives. Letters go to and fro among a whole cast of characters, events are reflected upon from very different angles, and the writer shifts in tone of voice and in judgement according to his or her present correspondent. Goethe does none of that. Apart from the Editor's interventions, the form of *Werther* is a one-sided correspondence. No letters are presented from Werther's main addressee, Wilhelm (a rather shadowy figure), nor are any of the notes Lotte wrote to Werther (we hear of a few) nor any more substantial communication from her. All replies of whatever kind to letters written by Werther must, we presume, have gone into the stove along with much else shortly before his death. Their absence is an ingredient of the fiction; but, before that, Goethe's suppression of them is a masterly violation of the epistolary novel's form.

The letter is an intrinsically dialogic form of writing. It addresses another person in the expectation or hope of a reply. Laclos's novel moves with great force and complexity in that dynamic of address and answer among half-a-dozen correspondents. In *Werther* there are no replies; effectively, in a dialogic form, the young man wanting correspondence conducts a monologue. He also keeps a diary; he alludes to it (p. 38), but we read nothing of it. That too must have gone into the flames. The diary's monologic form would certainly suit the increasingly solipsistic Werther. But as Goethe saw, it would be more expressive of his hero's situation and tragedy to choose a form implying dialogue and use it as a monologue. A one-sided correspondence—not a correspondence at all—is a telling image of Werther's fate. Much of what the novel is 'about' is realized in that master-stroke of form.

One-sidedness, a bad thing in a coroner accounting for a suicide, may be a good thing in a novelist, and in the case of Goethe's *Werther* most definitely is. The complex perspectivism of *Les Liaisons dangeureuses* gives the reader a bewildering number of slants on the story being told. That is not the same as 'a balanced view'. We don't go to novelists for a fair and balanced view of things but for the felt truth, however partial, of being human in particular circumstances. Laclos gives us a variety of perspectives; Goethe quite deliberately limits his. One-sidedness—an achievement, not a regrettable accident, of Goethe's chosen form—is a means to the truth of his hero's situation.

But what about the Editor? To a degree unprecedented in the tradition of the epistolary novel Goethe's Editor affects or seeks to affect the reader's reception of the story in which he is not otherwise a participant. He introduces himself as the diligent collator and presenter of everything he could find concerning Werther's life and death; as the story proceeds he adds the occasional rather pedantic footnote; and he appears in person again towards the end, regretting that the documentation has become fragmentary and telling us that he has done his level best—talking to those closely or at all involved—to gather and assess the facts and the different views of those facts. In that role or pose he sounds like a living corrective to one-sidedness, as though we might expect from him the balanced account. In practice he compromises his position at the outset. Having said that he has gathered together and now lays before us all he could find on the subject of 'poor Werther', he continues: 'and I know that you will thank me. His mind and his character will compel your admiration and your love, and his fate will compel your tears.' The Editor offers us Werther as an object of admiration, love, and pity, and commends 'this little book' to any reader 'feeling driven as he was', as a comforter and a friend. That is not neutral.

The curious marker of this partiality is the occasional elision of the role of the Editor into that of third-person omniscient narrator. Viewed strictly, in keeping with his stated office, he can only know what is in Werther's recovered letters, two being to Lotte, the rest to Wilhelm, and whatever else he has learned from anyone he approached in his researches—talking to them he may get some idea of what thoughts and feelings were at play in the chief characters. In practice he grossly exceeds the brief and scope that any such investigative procedures might have given him. He forgets himself—or Goethe does—and becomes at times, in effect, an omniscient narrator. For example:

Even as he walked, his thoughts turned to this subject. 'Oh yes,' he said to himself, grinding his teeth—'Close, friendly, tender, and sympathetic in all his dealings with her, a lasting peaceful fidelity! Complacent satisfaction, that's what it is, and indifference. Does not any wretched piece of business engage him more than the woman who is so precious? Does he know how fortunate he is? Can he value her as she deserves? He has her—well then, he has her—I know that, just as I know other things, I believe I have got used to the thought, it will still drive me mad, it will still be the death of me—And has his friendship to me held good? Does he not think my devotion to Lotte a trespass on his rights and my attentiveness to her a silent reproach? I know it full well, I feel it, he does not like to see me, he wishes me removed, my presence is irksome to him.'

Since Werther is alone, this can only be a—quite plausible— monologue invented by the Editor/Narrator. He does the same for Lotte (pp. 95–6): she is alone with her very troubled thoughts which it is not likely she shared as documentary evidence with the diligent Editor. Really, the Editor seems not able to resist the pull into omniscience at those moments when he feels the story needs it. He becomes a narrator, an agent of the fiction, close to the author, driven deeper and deeper by the force of imaginative sympathy. Hard to know whether Goethe in the passion of the first writing of *Werther* even noticed this sliding. I doubt if his first readers did, or cared a jot about it if they did. And when Goethe revised the novel more than a decade later he not only let that mixing of editor with narrator stand, he made further use of it, actually to dwell on Lotte's inner trouble in the passage alluded to above and to adjust the feelings readers might have about Albert.

Allowing the Editor to be pulled out of his role into a narrative sympathy with Werther's life is of a piece with presenting, in an epistolary novel, only Werther's side of the correspondence. Both are expressive techniques. Goethe wrote—made sentences, devised narrative strategies—to ensure that Werther's story would be *compelling*. The Editor reverts to his proper role in the final pages. He says only what he could plausibly have got from witnesses. And from the writerly point of view that too is apt and telling:

He died at twelve noon. The presence of the Land Steward and the measures he took hushed up any public outcry. At night towards eleven he had him buried in the place he had chosen for himself. The old man followed the coffin with his sons, Albert could not do it. They feared for Lotte's life. Working-men carried him. No priest attended. (pp. 111–12)

The Two Versions

In his letter of 15 August Werther extrapolates the following out of his experience of telling stories to Lotte's brothers and sisters:

It has taught me that an author who publishes an altered version of his story must necessarily harm the work, however poetically improved it may be. The first impression finds us willing, human beings are made to be persuaded of the most outlandish things—but they hit home in us and stick so fast, woe betide anyone trying to erase or eradicate them. (p. 44)

Goethe retained that passage when he revised *Werther* for publication in 1787. Rather like the allusion to Werther's diary in this novel composed of letters, it is—or after the revision becomes—a self-conscious comment on authorial freedom and ought to deter us from thinking that the second version fixes the truth of the story more definitively than the first.

Comparison of the two versions, tracking and commenting on the changes, is unavoidably bedevilled by the mixing of fiction and biography discussed above. As soon as he read *Werther*, Kestner objected to the characterization of Lotte and Albert, and Goethe promised him he would do something about it within a year for a new edition. Taken at face value that would mean the author had intended his fiction to be a fair account of a situation he and his friends had been in and was prepared to try again to be fairer. It is certainly the case that one strain in the rewriting (through the agency of the Editor greatly exceeding his role) does make Albert more sympathetic. But another, going deeper into the unspoken feelings of Lotte, suggests just as strongly as in 1774 that Werther has grounds for believing, after the reading of Ossian, that she loves him. The second version of *Werther* is not more balanced than the first—balance, as I said earlier, is not what novelists are after—but in the course of the rewriting Goethe slanted his interests differently, he saw aspects he could emphasize or develop but not, I think, to soothe the feelings of Christian and Charlotte Kestner.

For one thing, Goethe did not reissue *Werther* within a year, as he had promised. Not until 30 April 1780 did he even reread it (and marvel at it), and only two years after that did he consider revision. Oddly enough, he had no copy of the first and authorized edition of 1774 to hand. Instead, in June 1782 he borrowed a pirated and unfaithful edition of 1775 (Himburg, Berlin) from Charlotte von Stein, had it copied, and entered his alterations into that manuscript. He wrote to Kestner about it in May 1783; took no notice whatsoever of his wish that Lotte at the ball should behave differently; and completed the revision in the summer of 1786, just before he fled to Italy, breaking with Charlotte, ending their long involvement. This second version of *Werther* appeared in 1787 in Volume 1 of an eight-volume edition of Goethe's works published by Göschen in Leipzig, a single-volume edition of it appearing later that year.

Both versions of *Werther* are in two halves. Both begin with the same address to the reader by the Editor, who in both is the collector and presenter of the material. The chief addition to the second version is the story of the farmhand so driven by love that he commits murder. He joins other figures already in the novel as another reflection of or slant on Werther. His story is told in the new letters 30 May and 4 September; while the Editor now takes over the narrative after 6 December (not 17 December as in the first version) to tell us more about Werther and the farmhand. Beyond that, Goethe wrote half-a-dozen more letters, mostly very short, and made short additions to three others. And he redated three letters, without significantly changing the text.

Overall, in his revision Goethe widened and varied the perspective his readers might have on Werther, his chief agent in this being the Editor, who now exceeds his strict role and function even more than in the earlier version. One example may stand for many to show what shifts in our view of the Werther–Lotte–Albert triangle Goethe made possible through his revision. In the first version the Editor makes this comment, as though with complete authority, on Albert's relationship with his wife Lotte: 'little by little his amicable dealings with her took second place to his work.' In the second version Werther mutters the same judgement in a soliloquy the Editor could not possibly have overheard: 'Does not any wretched piece of business engage him more than the woman who is so precious?' Neither has any greater objective status than the other; but the second converts the verdict from a pseudo-fact (passed on by an omniscient narrator) into Werther's opinion ascribed to him by the same narrator.

In the 1787 version this Editor/Narrator spends more time on Lotte's feelings, both for Albert and for Werther, and though his brief (as we might call it) is to shore up her marriage more firmly he also, in a truthful counter-tendency, makes clearer what she has in Werther and does not wish to lose. Fortifying the marriage, Goethe added two paragraphs to the Editor's account of Lotte's state, just after the letter of 20 December (pp. 90–1), in addition deleting some suggestions of real hostility and resentment between husband and wife concerning Werther. In the first version, for example, Albert seems to set off on his business trip only when he has heard from Lotte that Werther will not call: 'Lotte, who knew very well that he had for a long time been postponing this business and that it would keep him away from home for a night, understood the pantomime all too well and was deeply troubled by it.' In the second version, omitting the above, Goethe—through his

Editor/Narrator—affirms the marriage: 'She saw herself joined eternally to a man whose love and fidelity she knew, to whom she was deeply devoted, whose calm and reliability seemed sent by heaven to be the grounds on which a good woman could build her life's happiness, and she felt what he would always be to her and to her children' (p. 95). And in the first version, when Werther arrives unexpectedly after this, it is in part to defy Albert and in anger at his suspicions that she allows Werther to stay and suggests that he read to her: 'She pondered the situation for a while until the feeling of her innocence rose up in her with some pride. She would defy Albert and his foolish ideas, and firm in the purity of her own heart . . .'

When Albert comes home, Lotte—in the first version—finds his presence 'for the first time quite unbearable', because of the muddle of feelings she is in. Told of Werther's visit, Albert comments sarcastically, 'He chooses his moment'. In the second version Goethe omits both of these very overt expressions and spends longer explaining the unhappy state husband and wife will be in when Werther's servant comes to borrow the pistols. In so doing, he makes explicit at least the question of their complicity in his suicide:

How heavily—though at that moment she could not see it—the constraint lay upon her which had settled between the two of them. Good and sensible people had, because of certain secret differences, ceased to talk to one another, each brooded on their own rightness and the other's wrongness and things became so fraught and complicated that at precisely the critical moment on which all depended it was impossible to untie the knot. Had they before now by some happy intimacy been brought close again, had a mutual love and understanding come alive between them and opened their hearts, perhaps our friend might still have been saved. (p. 106)

In the second version, as the Editor dwells more on Lotte's situation, he makes clear (see pp. 95–6) how unwilling she is to give Werther up; while the description of what the reading of Ossian does to her and to him is—but for a few details of orthography—carried over verbatim from the first to the second version. In brief, the revision of *Werther* in no way reduces the claims of the relationship between Lotte and Werther. Indeed, by affirming the marriage, by making Albert more sympathetic and Lotte's devotion to him indisputable, Goethe actually intensifies the tension she lives in. The Editor in his amplified role makes it clear that she does want Werther in her life.

Most of the correction, redirection, and amplification is done through the Editor/Narrator in the final stages of the novel. But at least one among the short additions to the corpus of Werther's letters—that of 12 September—surely shows Lotte playing knowingly with his feelings; as does also perhaps—from 5 September—the fond note to her husband that she leaves lying around. These additions rather strengthen the sense already there in letters of 13 and 16 July in Book One and 21 November in Book Two that Werther has grounds for his assertion: 'She loves me!'

Consistently in revising *Werther* Goethe moderated or removed the more obvious markers in orthography, vocabulary, and syntax of his *Sturm und Drang*. This certainly affects the tone of the novel and might for a reader well enough attuned to that early period feel like a cooling down. But most modern readers—in German or in English—won't feel much diminution. The passion of the work survives the lessening of its period accent.

A Novel in Two Books

Telling the story of *Werther* as he does, Goethe, like other epistolary novelists, deliberately induces a sense that the book has no author but is the work of an editor who presents the documents he has gathered. But authorship, purposely subordinated there, is very apparent in the whole shape of the novel, most obviously in its division into two Books. Deciding on that simple structure, Goethe in 1774, and even more so in 1787, exploited it to very good effect. Being offered the story in two almost equal halves, the reader is bound to compare and contrast figures, encounters, and events either side of the caesura, especially recurrences. It is a strategy of both counterpoint and counterpart, the purpose of which is to bring home to us more fully and more variously Werther's situation and his progress into suicide.

For example, in Book One, soon after setting himself up in Wahlheim, Werther meets the schoolmaster's daughter and her three children. Her husband is away in Switzerland seeking to secure a legacy. Werther, having sketched two of the children, converts their mother into the very image of bucolic contentment. In Book Two he meets the woman again: her youngest child has died, her husband has come home ill and destitute.

Again, in Book One Werther meets the farmhand and is moved by his passionate attachment to the woman who employs him. Werther 'idolizes' him. In Book Two the farmhand murders his rival, Werther appropriates him as an alter ego, both heading into death. (The farmhand doubles with the clerk driven mad by love for Lotte, and both marshal Werther the way that he was going.)

In Book One Werther, visiting the pastor with Lotte, praises and blesses the parsonage's walnut trees—for their beauty, for the pleasure they give, for the connection they uphold with previous incumbents. In Book Two the new Pastor's wife has them cut down.

In these three instances the images—made by Werther—turn across the caesura of the two books from good to ill. A similar alteration, not quite so obvious, occurs when Werther abandons Homer, his companion in Book One, for Ossian who conducts him into death.

Book One opens with one departure—Werther has left his friend Wilhelm and the young woman Leonore who had fallen in love with him—and closes with another: he tears himself away from Lotte and Albert. In the course of Book Two Werther leaves his employment, leaves the Prince's estate, returns to his native town, returns to Lotte and Albert, and after twice telling Wilhelm 'I'd be better if I left', departs into suicide. Werther fools around with Albert's pistol in Book One, uses it in earnest in Book Two; justifies suicide in One, commits it in Two.

Figures, motifs, particular localities, entire landscapes are used in this fashion to demonstrate how unstably dependent upon Werther's mind the outside world is. Like Shelley (quoting Milton), Goethe's Werther knows that 'the mind is its own place, and in itself | Can make a Heaven of Hell, a Hell of Heaven'. Werther, rather like the Magnetic Mountain he refers to in the letter of 26 July, draws things and people to him, but as reflections of himself, so that they become baleful as his state worsens.

The Triangle

Most obviously *Werther* is an unhappy love story. Werther falls in love with a woman at first 'as good as engaged to' and then indeed married to another man. The two men, though very different in character, do, for a while at least, like and esteem each other; and Werther and Lotte have in common much that matters. At the heart of tragedy there is always loss and a sense of waste, and that is certainly the case here. Good things, instead of nourishing pres-ent lives, go the way of death instead. Lotte, between the two men, quite understandably wants both of them—and wants them to be friends. As Werther observes (30 July): 'Women are subtle in things of that sort, and rightly. If she can keep two admirers on good terms with one another—not many could!—it will always be to her advantage.' Hence her wishful thinking: 'Oh, if . . . she could have changed him into a brother how happy she would have been!—or had she been free to marry him to one of her friends she might have hoped to restore his relationship with Albert wholly to what it was' (p. 95). But she can't think of any of her friends who is good enough for Werther, and in her heart of hearts she knows very well that her feelings for him are more than sisterly. She knows what she needs for her life's fulfilment and knows she won't get it.

Werther is a social novel. It deals in realist mode with the lives people live—are permitted to live—under a particular social order. Werther's thwarting in love must be seen in the context of a larger frustration and denial. In old age Goethe remarked to his chron-icler Eckermann: 'The much-talked-of "Age of Werther" . . . belongs in truth not to the course of world culture but to the course through life of every individual who, born with a sense of freedom and naturalness, must find his place and learn to accommodate himself in the constraining structures of an

outdated world.'[1] In the novel Werther himself is the chief casu-
alty, but Lotte, just as important, is also seriously damaged. 'They
feared for Lotte's life' (p. 112)—quite rightly, as they might fear
for the lives of the many women living in such constraint. Dying,
Lotte's mother binds her to her father on terms like those of a
marriage: 'be faithful and obedient to your father, like a wife'
(p. 51); and having done that, she commends her, as wife-to-be,
to Albert. Lotte is bound into motherhood and the duties of a wife,
looking after eight brothers and sisters and her father, before the
second contract, to Albert, becomes operative. This was not then
an unusual fate for an elder daughter. Goethe witnessed it at close
hand in Charlotte Buff, and saw something similar in Maximiliane
von La Roche's marriage to Brentano. His character Lotte accepts
it and, but for Werther, might never have felt herself constrained
and denied. Two years after the publication of *Werther* came the
American Declaration of Independence and the words: 'We hold
these truths to be self-evident, that all men are created equal, that
they are endowed by their Creator with certain unalienable Rights,
that among these are Life, Liberty and the pursuit of Happiness.'
That famous Preamble was not plucked out of thin air. The words
took that irrevocable shape because the times, in the writings of
poets, novelists, and *philosophes*, had for a while been demanding
it. And the rights were not only unalienable, they were also not to
be restricted. Goethe, in 1774 concentrating on his young male
hero, necessarily also asked: What hope do women have in the
pursuit of happiness?

Consider in that light Friederike, the young woman constrained
by her jealous and sulky lover (1 July); the wife who only by a
subterfuge can run the household of her skinflint husband (11
July); Fräulein B. in whom Werther discerns a kindred spirit, the
life in her choked by the social order, her embittered and tyran-
nical aunt (16 March); the Pastor's shrivelled wife who hates the
walnut trees (15 September); the wives and mothers in the Count's
circle whose whole identity resides in social rank (15 March); and
Werther's own mother who after the death of his father left the

---

[1] Eckermann, *Gespräche mit Goethe*, 2 Jan. 1824.

'beloved homely place and imprisoned herself in her unbearable town' (5 May).

Werther himself does not think all men equal and he knows what advantages his social class brings him. Nonetheless, he continually draws attention to constraint and unfreedom and complains bitterly when he suffers from them. Returning to his birthplace, he recalls with horror what school was like: 'I remembered the unease, the tears, the oppression of the feelings, the anxiety around the heart that I suffered in that hole' (9 May). He loves children and is easy with them, and enlists their state (and his own when he is with them) in a polemic against 'the prison-house' of adulthood; in his art too he upholds naturalness, against the rules. Altogether, he gets on easily with 'uncultured' people, they like him, confide in him, he associates their lives with the simplicity of Homeric or 'patriarchal' times, again in opposition to the unnaturalness of the modern middle and aristocratic classes. In his employment with the Envoy at the beginning of Book Two he feels himself to be oppressed and reduced and, finding in the Count and in Fräulein B. two exceptional people with whom it is possible to be more fully human, he soon falls foul of the social order itself, is humiliated, and driven further into the solitary obsession that will kill him. Werther—and anyone like him—would be bound to suffer in that society. Constraint and denial, inherent in the social order, become unbearable when he must suffer them also in his love for Lotte.

Under a social order which strictly regulates relations between the sexes those encounters that are permitted may become very highly charged. Two such in *Werther* are dancing and literature. By the time they reach the location of the dance in Book One (16 June) Werther is already in love with Lotte, and she has candidly admitted how much she loves dancing. Having waltzed with her he tells Wilhelm that he would not wish any woman he had a claim on to waltz with anyone else. He knows the sexual charge of that dance in particular. And the conventions allow it. Then, at the open window after the thunderstorm, Lotte puts her hand on his and utters one word, the poet's name: 'Klopstock!' Looking at a place—the garden—with Werther, she assumes they have also a common place in literature, a particular poem. There, as in the dance, it is permitted to meet.

Already bound by her mother to her father and his children, in the space before Albert returns and binds her by engagement and marriage to him she commits herself quite seriously to Werther, and he knows it. Her engagement and her marriage actually intensify their meetings—their sympathies—and to a point where it becomes harder and harder to keep them within the permitted limits. When at Lotte's suggestion (p. 96), as though it were the safest option, Werther reads aloud to her his translation of Ossian, that is a vastly enlarged and in practice vastly more dangerous equivalent of the spoken name and the remembered poem at the dance. After it, having kissed her, he knows she loves him and he hastens to die.

Goethe described his play *Torquato Tasso* (written 1788–90) as '*Werther* raised to a higher power'. Its hero, a poet, falls from favour at Court because he transgresses the bounds the Court has set for him. Catastrophe ensues when he tries to kiss the Princess, who requires him and his poetry to be a zone apart in which she can enjoy love platonically, which is to say cerebrally, and never act on it. His transgression is to want the thing itself, to enact poems in reality. Lotte—and she can hardly be blamed for it—tries, like the Princess Leonore with Tasso, to confine herself and Werther to books and talk and the deep companionship of their sympathies. Sensibly married to Albert, for her full self-realization she also needs Werther, and she struggles to imagine a form—him as her brother or married to a friend of hers or getting on well with Albert—in which that might be possible. Literature, the zone that is permitted and might be thought safe, only hurries them into catastrophe.

Lotte, when Werther meets her, admits to once having enjoyed romantic novels (p. 19); but latterly, so busy with her family, she much prefers those that depict a world like her own. The former, so attractive to many reading women, extend the imagination beyond its domestic confines. The latter are safe books, they resign a woman to where and how she must live. Werther drags her from there into the exotic threnodies of Ossian.

Early on, before he has met Lotte, Werther, like Hamlet, views life as a prison but consoles himself with the thought that you can always break out of it. His defence of suicide to Albert (12 August) is only an amplification of that early casual remark. Which is almost to say that his one 'unalienable' freedom in that outdated social order is the freedom to kill himself. Self-realization, the attainment of an autonomous life, being denied him, he asserts himself, like Ottilie in *Elective Affinities*, by committing suicide. Never again did Goethe so consequentially pursue the individual's bid for autonomy in a society thwarting it. No other work of his (except *Urfaust*, written a couple of years earlier) moves so inexorably to a tragic end. After *Werther* he always, in the interests of continuing life, hedged, compromised, escaped into irony. But—*Elective Affinities* proves it—he knew very well how inimical to a fulfilled life certain orders of society are: he saw how they freeze, petrify, ossify the life in people, bring about what Elizabeth Bowen so well depicts: the death of the heart. A hundred years after *Werther*, in Fontane's *Effi Briest*, the denial of life still rules. Instetten, Effi's code-bound husband, says: 'We don't need to be happy. And the very last thing we have, is any *right* to be'—as though 'We hold these truths to be self-evident...' had never been broadcast through the world.

The Reception of Werther

Goethe wrote *Werther* because he had to; and in that 'having to' was the desire to be rid of the novel's material, to liberate himself from an entangled and painful phase of his own life. Again and again he would use his writing in this way, cathartically, to get clear. Having finished *Werther*, he felt, he said 'as after a general confession, joyous and free and entitled to a new life'.[1] There can hardly ever have been a greater discrepancy between the author's interest and that of the reading public.

There were about thirty reprints of the 1774 version (most of them pirated) by 1790, and about twenty-five of the 1787 version before Goethe's death in 1832. And, of course, numerous

[1] Goethe, *Dichtung und Wahrheit*, part 3, book 13.

translations: the first French 1775, the first English (via the French) 1779, Italian two years later. And in German and in the languages of the translations scores of adaptations, fictional critiques, poetical responses, and sequels. In 1775, for example, a German version retold the story from Lotte's point of view. And in England, in 1786, one William James, exploiting the market, produced a *Letters of Charlotte during her Connexion with Werter*, in two volumes, exactly the same format as the original. 'I am confident,' he wrote, 'that a collection of nonsense under the same title would at least sell an edition.' England, quite as much as Germany, went Werthermad. At Mrs Salmon's Royal Historical Wax-Work in Fleet Street you could see the 'Group of the Death of Werter, attended by Charlotte and her Family'. In scores of literary, plastic, and musical forms Werther's life was extended in Europe and America and even into China (where a porcelain factory reproduced him on tea-sets for the European market). Men dressed like him, in blue coat, buff-yellow waistcoat and knee-breeches, women wore a perfume called 'Eau de Werther'. Christel von Lassberg drowned herself in Weimar's river Ilm 16 January 1778 with a copy of *Werther* in her pocket, to Goethe's great distress. He felt for people—there were many—whom the novel did not liberate as it had him but drove them deeper into their own dangers. On the other hand, *Werther* was one of Napoleon's favourite books (Goethe discussed a certain passage with him), and Frankenstein's monster 'found in it a never-ending source of speculation and astonishment'.

The general public and Goethe's fellow writers in the *Sturm und Drang* received *Werther* with an extreme and often lachrymose enthusiasm. Some churchmen and some rationalists, however, anathematized it, and seeing so many carried away felt they must answer back. Such were, for example, the writer and critic Friedrich Nicolai, who wrote a correction in the form of a *Freuden des jungen Werthers* ('Joys of Young Werther': Albert kindly and reasonably cedes Lotte to Werther), and the Hamburg pastor Goeze who, from the pulpit of the city's newspapers, prophesied that *Werther* would usher in a new Sodom and Gomorrah. Leipzig banned the book altogether, and with it the wearing of the Werther costume. In the general welter of the novel's immorality—the hero's

idleness, his and Lotte's undermining of the institution of marriage, and so on—worst of all for the churchmen was what they
understood as its justification, even celebration, of suicide. Karl
Wilhelm Jerusalem had himself defended the act, and with the
muddling of biography and fiction so characteristic of the writing
and the reading of *Werther* some critics assumed that not only the
hero but also his author were doing the same. True, the book does
very powerfully demonstrate how a person may get into a tunnel
of vision that will end in self-slaughter; but that is the job of fiction: to make palpable various ways of being human, be they good
or ill. There is enough in *Werther*—even in the first version—to
prevent any attentive reader from supposing it glorifies suicide.
Werther's arguments in his discussion of the subject with Albert
(12 August) are all over the place; passages in his final letter to
Lotte are hysterical; his death is messy in the extreme; and he
inflicts on the woman he loves and on the man who was his friend
a Christmas gift of grief and guilt. The book ends not in apothe-
osis but in implacable horror.

Goethe never did get rid of Werther. Having completed his
revision of the novel, he bolted to Italy and tried to live there
incognito, as Filippo Miller, a German painter, but was frequently
recognized as himself and the author of *Werther*. In March 1787
the English botanist James Edward Smith noted him at a soirée in
the house of Sir William Hamilton in Naples as 'M. von Goethe,
prime minister to the duke of Saxe Weimar, author of the well
known Sorrows of Werter', which two capacities Goethe was des-
perately seeking to shed. But of course it was not just a reputation
fixed on him by an uncomprehending public. Werther truly was an
alter ego, a possibility which Goethe acknowledged in himself and
fought with, to stay alive. He reincarnated him in the poet Tasso;
and in 1824, suffering an unhappy love for a girl scarcely older
than Maximiliane von la Roche (long since dead) had been in
1772, 'celebrated' a fiftieth-anniversary new publication of *Werther*
with a poem addressed to that 'much-lamented shade' and with
rueful reference to his own present plight. Werther the character,
Werther the novel, works of fiction, were recognized at once and
are still recognized as facts of life.

NOTE ON THE TRANSLATION

For this translation, which is of the second version of *Die Leiden des jungen Werthers* (1787), I have used the text in Volume 6 of the Hamburg Edition of Goethe's works, edited by Erich Trunz. His notes and commentary and the documents assembled there were extremely useful to me, as was also the volume of *Erläuterungen und Dokumente* (No. 8113), edited by Kurt Rothmann, which accompanies the Reclam *Werther*. I gratefully acknowledge the work of those two scholars.

My working method was, as always, not to consider any previous translations until I had finished and felt sure of the character and slant of my own. Then, checking for lexical accuracy, I read very closely, and learned from, the translations done by Michael Hulse (Penguin, 1989), Catherine Hutter (Signet, 1962), and R. D. Boylan (Bohn's Standard Library, 1854). Boylan's was the first satisfactory *Werther* in English. Anyone interested in the earlier versions, and in the whole slow and suspicious reception of Goethe's writings into English, might like to consult the *Oxford History of Literary Translation in English*, vol. 4, edited by Kenneth Haynes and Peter France (Oxford University Press, 2005).

In the text, asterisks refer to Explanatory Notes. The numbered footnotes are Goethe's.

I am grateful to Helen Constantine and Sasha Dugdale who read and commented on my translation; to my editor Judith Luna who encouraged me to take on the work in the first place and gave me much helpful advice along the way; and to Jeff New for his meticulous and sensitive copy-editing.

SELECT BIBLIOGRAPHY

Editions of the German Texts of Werther

Paulin, Roger (ed.), *Die Leiden des jungen Werthers* (London: Bristol Classical Press, 1993). This is an edition, with a good preface, introduction, and notes in English, of the 1774 edition of Goethe's *Werther*. In two appendices it presents all the chief alterations and additions made by Goethe for the edition of 1787 as well as the full text of Kestner's report to Goethe on the life and death of Karl Wilhelm Jerusalem.

Lorenz, Annika, and Schmiedt, Helmut (eds.), *Die Leiden des jungen Werthers. Synoptischer Druck der beiden Fassungen 1774 und 1787* (Paderborn: Igel Verlag, 1997). This sets the two editions side by side on facing pages, which gives a very clear view of the changes Goethe made.

On Goethe and his Age

Boyle, Nicholas, *Goethe: The Poet and the Age*, Volume I: *1749–1790*; Volume II: *1790–1803* (Oxford: Oxford University Press, 1991 and 2000).

Bruford, W. H., *Germany in the Eighteenth Century* (Cambridge: Cambridge University Press, 1935; 1952).

——*Culture and Society in Classical Weimar, 1775–1806* (Cambridge: Cambridge University Press, 1962).

Fairley, Barker, *A Study of Goethe* (Oxford: Oxford University Press, 1947).

Friedenthal, Richard, *Goethe: His Life and Times* (London: Weidenfeld & Nicolson, 1965).

Gray, R. D., *Goethe: A Critical Introduction* (Cambridge: Cambridge University Press, 1967).

Graham, Ilse, *Goethe: Portrait of the Artist* (Berlin: De Gruyter, 1977)

Lewes, G. H., *The Life and Works of Goethe* (London, 1855; reissued in Everyman's Library: Dent, 1949).

Lukács, Georg, *Goethe and his Age* (London: Merlin Press, 1968).

Reed, T. J., *The Classical Centre: Goethe and Weimar 1775–1832* (Oxford: Oxford University Press, 1984).

Reed, T. J., *Goethe*, Past Masters Series (Oxford: Oxford University Press, 1984).

Sharpe, Lesley (ed.), *The Cambridge Companion to Goethe* (Cambridge: Cambridge University Press, 2002).

Swales, Martin, and Swales, Erika, *Reading Goethe: A Critical Introduction to the Literary Work* (London: Camden House, 2002).

Williams, John R., *The Life of Goethe: A Critical Biography* (Oxford: Blackwell's, 1998).

John Oxenford translated *Dichtung und Wahrheit* (as *The Autobiography of Goethe*) for Bohn in 1848; it was reissued in 1971. His translation of Eckermann's *Conversations with Goethe in the last Years of his Life* was reprinted by Dent (Everyman) in 1930.

On Werther and Goethe's Fiction

Atkins, Stuart, *The Testament of Werther in Poetry and Drama* (Cambridge, Mass.: Harvard University Press, 1949).

Blackall, Eric, *Goethe and the Novel* (New York: Cornell University Press, 1976).

Reiss, Hans, *Goethe's Novels* (London: Macmillan, 1969).

Swales, Martin, *Goethe: The Sorrows of Young Werther*, Landmarks of World Literature (Cambridge: Cambridge University Press, 1987).

Further Reading in Oxford World's Classics

Goethe, Johann Wolfgang von, *Elective Affinities*, trans. David Constantine.

—— *Erotic Poems*, trans. David Luke, intro. Hans Rudolf Vaget.

—— *Faust, Part One*, trans. David Luke.

—— *Faust, Part Two*, trans. David Luke.

A CHRONOLOGY OF JOHANN WOLFGANG VON GOETHE

1749   (28 Aug.) Goethe born into a well-to-do family in Frankfurt am Main.

1755   Lisbon Earthquake.

1756–63   Seven Years War.

1752–65   Goethe privately educated. He has tutors in French, Hebrew, Italian, and English. His early reading includes the poetry of Klopstock, Homer in translation, the Bible, and French Classical dramatists.

1765-8   At the University of Leipzig reading Law, and a good deal else. Friendships and love affairs (Käthchen Schönkopf), many poems in rococo style, his first comedies. First readings of Shakespeare.

1768   (8 June) Winckelmann, historian and enthusiastic apologist of Classical art, murdered in Trieste. (Aug. 1768–Mar. 1770) Goethe mostly at home in Frankfurt, often ill. Interest in alchemy, association with Pietists.

1770–1   Student in Strasbourg, in love with Friederike Brion, friendship with Herder, who directed him to folk-songs and ballads; reading Shakespeare, Ossian, and Homer. The breakthrough into his own poetic voice.

1771–4   In Frankfurt and Wetzlar. The first version of *Götz von Berlichingen*, a drama in 'Shakespearian' style, written in six weeks. Some legal, more literary activity. He writes the first poems of his *Sturm und Drang* ('Storm and Stress') period.

1772–5   (possibly even earlier) First phase of work on *Faust*.

1774   He writes and publishes *Die Leiden des jungen Werthers*. *Götz* staged in Berlin. Vast success of *Werther*.

1775   In love with Lili Schönemann, engagement to her. Journey to Switzerland. His drama *Egmont* begun. Invited to Weimar, to enter the service of Duke Karl August. Breaks off his engagement. November, arrives in Weimar and meets Charlotte von Stein, the wife of a Weimar Court official.

1776   American Declaration of Independence. Herder moves to Weimar. Goethe becomes a servant of the state. Interest in the silver mines in Ilmenau; beginnings of his geological studies.

1776–86   Increasingly engaged in duties of the state (ennobled 1782); journeys on business and for pleasure to the Harz Mountains, Berlin, and Switzerland; involvement with Charlotte von Stein; work for the Weimar theatre, scientific studies. Many poems, work on the novel *Wilhelm Meisters Lehrjahre* (*Wilhelm Meister's Apprentice Years*) and the plays *Iphigenie auf Tauris* and *Tasso*. He leaves works unfinished, he feels frustrated and confined.

1786   (Sept.) Sudden departure for Italy without informing the Duke or his friends (including Charlotte von Stein). Arrives in Rome, 29 October.

1786–8   In Italy: Rome, Naples, Sicily, Rome. Lives among artists under an assumed name; studies to become one. The making of his Classicism. *Iphigenie* is recast in verse. *Egmont* finished. Further work on *Tasso* and *Faust*.

1787   Publication of the revised version of *Werther*.

1788   (18 June) Back in Weimar. Released from most of his state duties. (12 July) Begins living with Christiane Vulpius, a young woman who worked in Weimar's artificial flower factory. (Sept.) The first of the *Roman Elegies*, which, in Classical style, celebrate love and Rome; work on *Tasso*.

1789   French Revolution. *Tasso* completed. (25 Dec.) Birth of a son, August, the only one of Christiane and Goethe's five children who survived infancy.

1790   (Mar.–June) Second Italian journey (to Venice), a disappointment. Publication of *Faust, ein Fragment* (*Faust: A Fragment*).

1791   Tom Paine, *The Rights of Man*.

1792   Goethe is present at the Battle of Valmy, with Duke Karl August, on the side of the Prussians against the Revolutionary armies of France.

1793   (21 Jan.) Execution of Louis XVI. (May–July) Goethe again
        accompanies Karl August and the Prussian army on cam-
        paign, being present at the Siege of Mainz.

1794   Beginning of Goethe's friendship and correspondence with
        Schiller.

1795   *Roman Elegies* published. Their eroticism gives offence.

1796   The verse epic *Hermann und Dorothea* and the novel *Wilhelm
        Meister's Apprentice Years* published.

1797   He and Schiller write *Kunstballaden*—which are more highly
        wrought and reflective than traditional ballads—among
        Goethe's being 'Die Braut von Korinth' (The Bride of
        Corinth) and 'Der Gott und die Bajadere' (The God and the
        Bayadere). Visits Switzerland again.

1797–1801 Most of the third phase of work on *Faust, Part I*. Some
        notes for *Faust, Part II*.

1798–9 Poems in Classical metres (including the unfinished epic
        Achilleis); renewed work on *Faust*.

1799   Schiller moves to Weimar.

1800–5 Poems, work on *Faust*, a great deal of scientific work.

1805   Death of Schiller. Goethe ill, withdrawn, depressed.

1806   Battle of Jena, defeat of the Prussians; French troops in
        Weimar; Goethe marries Christiane Vulpius.

1807–9 Relationship with the eighteen-year-old Minna Herzlieb. The
        novel *Elective Affinities* written, work on *Wilhelm Meisters
        Wanderjahre* (*Wilhelm Meister's Years of Travel*), which is to be
        the continuation of the *Apprentice Years*. Begins work on the
        autobiography *Dichtung und Wahrheit* (*Poetry and Truth*).
        Received by Napoleon, admirer of *Werther*, who awards him
        the Cross of the Legion of Honour.

1808   *Faust, Part I* published.

1812   Meets Beethoven. The French retreat from Moscow.

1815   Battle of Waterloo.

1814–18 Relationship with Marianne von Willemer, wife of a
        Frankfurt banker; work on the *West-östlicher Divan*
        (*West-Eastern Divan*), an abundant collection, inspired by
        the fourteenth-century Persian poet Hafiz and by Marianne
        (and incorporating some of her poems).

1816   (6 June) Death of Christiane.

1816–17   Publication of the *Italian Journey*, put together from his notes, diaries, and letters of 1786–8.

1821   *Wilhelm Meister's Years of Travel* published.

1821–9   Greek War of Liberation.

1823–4   In love with the nineteen-year-old Ulrike von Levetzow. Parting from her unhappily, he writes *Trilogie der Leidenschaft*, one of the three poems being 'An Werther' ('To Werther'). From 1823, conversations with Johann Peter Eckermann, who will publish them after Goethe's death.

1824   Death of Byron.

1825–31 Continuing work on *Faust, Part II*.

1830   Revolution in France; the July Monarchy.

1832   (22 March) Death of Goethe. *Faust, Part II* published in December.

THE SORROWS OF
YOUNG WERTHER

Everything I could discover about poor Werther's story I have diligently gathered together and lay it before you now and know that you will thank me. His mind and his character will compel your admiration and your love, and his fate will compel your tears.

And you, amiable soul, feeling driven as he was, draw comfort from his suffering and let this little book be your friend if by chance or by some fault of your own you can find none nearer.

BOOK ONE

How glad I am to be away! My dear friend, what a thing the human heart is! I leave you, whom I love so much, from whom I was inseparable, and I am glad! You will forgive me, I know. Were not all my other dealings with people expressly designed by Fate to alarm and distress a heart like mine? Poor Leonore!* And yet I was innocent. Could I help it that whilst her charming and heedless sister was amusing me, a real passion was forming in poor Leonore's heart? And yet—am I wholly innocent? Did I not foster her feelings? Was I not myself delighted by the wholly truthful expressions of her nature, which, though not in the least laughable, so often made us laugh, and did I not—? But what sense is there in berating ourselves? My dear friend, I promise you I will mend my ways and cease forever chewing over the small evils that Fate puts in our path. I will enjoy the present and be done with the past. Dear friend, you are quite right, there would be less pain among people if they would desist—God knows what makes them do it—from so busily employing their imaginations in remembering past ills rather than in enduring an indifferent present.

I'd be grateful if you would tell my mother that I shall do my very best in her affair and that I'll write to her about it just as soon as I can. I've spoken to my aunt* and found her not at all the wicked woman our family makes her out to be. She is lively, spirited, and very good-hearted. I explained my mother's grievances over the portion of the inheritance being withheld; she told me her grounds, the reasons, and the conditions on which she would be prepared to release everything, and more than we were asking for.—In brief, I don't want to write about it now: tell my mother all will be well. And in this small matter, my friend, I have realized once again that misunderstandings and lethargy can cause more going wrong in the world than cunning and wickedness do. At least, those two are certainly less common.

Beyond that, I very much like being here, in this paradisal part of the country solitude is a precious balm for my heart, and that heart, so often struck cold, is warmed by the youthful season in all abundance. Every tree, every hedge is a bouquet of blossom. Oh to be a maybug and flit where you like in that sea of scents and get all your nourishment there!

The town itself is disagreeable but all around the beauty of nature is beyond expression. This induced the late Count M.* to lay out his garden on one of the numerous hills that in lovely variations cross their courses here, forming the sweetest valleys. The garden is simple and you feel the moment you enter that it was designed not by a scientific gardener but by a feeling heart desiring to enjoy itself. In the dilapidated little summer-house that was once his favourite place and is now mine, I have wept more than once in memory of the dead man. I'll soon be the lord of the garden. After only these few days the gardener is well disposed towards me—and he won't be the loser by it.

10 May

A wonderful cheerfulness has taken complete possession of my soul, like the beautiful spring mornings that I am enjoying so wholeheartedly. I am alone and am glad of my life in this locality made for souls like mine. My dear friend, I am so happy and have sunk so deep into the feeling of calm existence that my art suffers under it. I couldn't do a drawing now, not a line of one, and yet was never a greater artist than I am in these moments. When the moisture rises in a mist in the sweet valley all around me and the high sun rests on the surface of the forest's impenetrable darkness and only occasional beams find their way into the inner sanctum and I lie in the tall grass by the tumbling stream and, thus close to the earth, become aware of the myriad varieties of grasses, and when I feel the seething of the world of small things among the stalks, feel against my heart the countless unfathomable shapes and forms of the tiny creatures that flit and crawl, and I feel the presence of the Almighty who created us in his image, the wafting breath of the Love that encompasses all, that upholds and sustains us in an eternal joy, oh my friend, at the dawning then before my eyes when the world and the heavens reside in my soul completely like the bodily shape of a beloved woman, then how I yearn and often have said to myself, Oh could you give that some answering expression, only breathe into the page what is so fully and warmly alive in you till it becomes the mirror of your soul just as your soul is the mirror of the unending deity!—Oh my friend!—But it will be the downfall of me, I lie defeated by the force of the splendour of these phenomena.

12 May

I can't tell whether deceiving spirits hover over this locality or whether it is the warm and heavenly imagination of my heart that makes everything around me so paradisal. Just outside the town there is a well*—to which I am in thrall like Melusina* and her sisters.—You descend a small incline and find yourself at a cupola below which perhaps twenty steps go down to where an utterly clear water bubbles up out of marble. The low wall making an enclosure at the top, the tall overshadowing trees all round, the coolness of the place, it draws me and gives me the shivers too. No day goes by without my sitting there an hour. The girls come from the town to fetch water, the most innocent and the most necessary of tasks that formerly the very daughters of kings used to perform. As I sit there, the patriarchal idea comes to life very vividly in me, how they, the forefathers, would meet and become acquainted and courtships would begin* and how kind the spirits are that hover around wells and springs. Oh, anyone who after a long summer walk has ever refreshed himself at the coolness of a well must feel as I do.

13 May

You ask should you send me my books?—For heaven's sake, my dear friend, do no such thing! I have no wish to be directed, encouraged, fired up, any more. My heart is in quite enough ferment of itself. I need lulling, and I have had that in abundance from my Homer.* How often he has helped me calm the upheaval of my blood, for nothing you have ever encountered is quite so uneven and unsteady as this heart of mine. But I don't need to tell you that, since you, my dear friend, have so often had the burden of watching me shift from sorrow to extravagance and from sweet melancholy to harmful passion. But I tend my heart now like a sick child; grant its every wish. Keep that to yourself—there are people who would begrudge it me.

15 May

The common people hereabouts know me now and like me, especially the children. A sad thing struck me. At first when I approached them and asked them in a friendly way about this or that, some thought I had a mind to make fun of them and put me off very coarsely. I did not let that grieve me but I felt very keenly what I have often remarked: people of a certain social standing will always keep themselves coldly at a distance from the lower orders as though they feared any rapprochement might diminish them; and then there are flighty characters and evil jokers who make a show of abasing themselves only so that their superiority may be all the more painfully apparent to the poor.

I know very well that we are not equal, nor can we be; but in my view anyone who feels it necessary to keep away from the so-called common herd to make them respect him is as much at fault as a coward who keeps himself hidden from his enemy for fear of defeat.

The other day I came to the well and found a young maidservant who had put down her pitcher on the bottom step and was looking round for one of her friends to come and help her lift it on to her head. I went down and addressed her.—'Shall I help you, young lady?'—She blushed and blushed.—'Oh no, sir,' she said.—'Come now.'—She adjusted the coil of cloth on her head and I helped her. She thanked me and climbed the steps.

17 May

I have made all manner of acquaintances but have found no real company yet. I don't know what it is about me that attracts people; so many like me and attach themselves to me and I'm sorry then when our paths very soon diverge. If you ask me what the people here are like, I'm bound to say: as they are everywhere. Human beings are much of a muchness. Most spend the greater part of their time working in order to live, and what bit of freedom they are left with makes them so anxious they strive by all available means to be rid of it. What a thing it is to be human!

But all in all they are a decent crowd. Sometimes if I forget myself and enjoy, as human beings still may, the pleasures of sitting and jesting in all openness and conviviality around a nicely laid table or of arranging a ride or a dance when it suits, such things have a very good effect on me—just so long as I suppress any thought of the many other powers in me that are decaying unused and that I must take care to conceal. Oh, it constrains my heart!—But to be misunderstood is the fate of our kind.

Alas that the friend of my youth* has gone—alas that I ever knew her. I might say to myself, you are a fool, you are searching for something which is not to be found on earth. But I found her, I felt the heart and the generous soul of her in whose presence I felt myself to be more than I was because I was everything I could be. Dear God, did even one of the powers of my soul go unused then? In her company could I not open up all of the wonderful faculty of feeling with which my heart comprehends Nature? Our conversation was a ceaseless weaving of the finest sensibilities, and in the play of our wits, going further and further, even to the point of licence, we expressed our unique selves. And now!—Oh, the years she had ahead of me brought her sooner to the grave. I shall never forget her—her steadfastness, her heavenly patience.

A few days ago I met a person by the name of V., a candid young man with a very agreeable face. He is fresh from the academies, doesn't exactly think himself wise but does believe he knows more than others do. And he is hardworking, as was apparent in all manner of things. In brief, he is admirably knowledgeable. When he heard that I do a lot of sketching and know Greek (two great wonders hereabouts) he addressed himself to me and raked up a whole load of learning, from Batteux to Wood, from

de Piles to Winckelmann*, and informed me that he had read
Sulzer's *Theory** (the first part) and that he owned a manuscript
by Heyne* on the subject of Antiquity. I let him be.

And I have got to know another good man, the Duke's Land
Steward,* an open and honest person. They say it delights one's
soul to see him among his children, nine of them. People set particular store by his eldest daughter. He invited me to visit him and
I shall do so as soon as possible. He lives in the Duke's hunting
lodge, an hour and a half from here. He was allowed to move there
after the death of his wife, when being here at his residence in the
town became too painful for him.

Otherwise a few bizarre individuals have come my way about
whom everything is insufferable, above all their demonstrations of
friendship.

Adieu! You'll be happy with this letter, it is nothing but facts.

22 May

It has seemed to many that the life of man is only a dream, and I
am myself always accompanied by that feeling. When I consider
how narrowly the active and enquiring powers of a human being
are confined; when I see that all effective effort has as its end the
satisfaction of needs which themselves have no purpose except to
lengthen the duration of our poor existence, and that any contentment on one point or another of our enquiries consists only in
a sort of dreaming resignation as we paint the walls within which
we sit out our imprisonment with bright figures and vistas of
light—All that, Wilhelm, renders me speechless. I go back into
myself and find a whole world! Again, more in intimations and a
dark desire than in realization and living force. And everything
swims before my senses and I smile at the world and continue my
dreaming.

All our learned schoolmasters and tutors are agreed that children do not know why they want what they want. But no one likes
to think—blindingly obvious though it is, in my view—that
grown-ups too, like the children, totter around on the earth and,
like the children, do not know where they have come from or where

they are going, act no more than children do for any true purpose and are just as governed by biscuits, cakes, and the rod.

I don't mind telling you, since I know what your response will be, that I think those the happiest who, like children, live for the moment, trail their dolls around, dress them and undress them, tiptoe with great respect around the drawer in which Mama hides the sweet things they desire—then snatch, gobble, and cry for more.—They are happy creatures. And just as well off are those who give splendid names to their miserable occupations or, worse, to their passions, and proclaim them to be the works of giants, for the prosperity and salvation of mankind.—Yes, you are well off if you can live like that! But whoever in his humility knows what it all amounts to, who sees how every comfortable householder prinks up his little garden into a paradise and how doggedly even the unhappy man hauls himself and his burden further along the way, and that their one interest is the same: to view the light of the sun a minute more—seeing that, you are quiet and out of your own self you too may fashion a world of your own and even be happy in being human. And then, confined as you are, you harbour the sweet feeling of freedom in your heart and are conscious that you can always leave this prison* when you like.

26 May

You've long known my habit of settling in somewhere, setting up home in some cosy place and lodging there in all simplicity and frugality. Here too I have discovered an attractive spot.

About an hour from here there is a place called Wahlheim.[1]* It is very interestingly situated, on a hill, and if you follow the path up from the village you can encompass the whole valley in one view. A landlady there, not young any more but agreeable and cheerful, serves wine, beer, coffee; best are two lime trees whose wide-spreading branches overreach the little square outside the church; and enclosing all are farmhouses, barns, and yards. I've rarely come across a place so closely congenial and homely as this.

[1] Readers should not go looking for the places mentioned in these letters. We have thought it necessary to change their real names.

I have my table and chair fetched out from the house, and there I drink my coffee and read my Homer. On my first visit, coming by chance one lovely afternoon under those trees, the place felt quite deserted. They were all in the fields, there was only a boy of about four sitting on the ground and holding another, perhaps six months old, between his legs and against his chest so that he made a sort of armchair for him, and there he sat entirely peaceably though his black eyes looked around in very lively fashion. The scene pleased me: I sat down opposite, on a plough, and sketched that brotherly pose with great pleasure. I added the nearest fence, a barn door, and one or two broken wagon wheels, just as they were ranged together, and found after an hour that I had made a very interesting and harmonious sketch without introducing the least thing of my own. This strengthened me in my resolve henceforth to hold only to Nature. She alone is infinitely rich and she alone can make the great artist. One can say a good deal in favour of the rules, roughly what one can say in favour of civil society. A person shaping himself after the rules will never produce anything that is tasteless or bad, just as a man who lets himself be formed by the law and by decorum will never be an intolerable neighbour or a remarkable miscreant; but say what you like, all rules destroy the true feeling of Nature and the true expression of Nature. You'll tell me that is too severe! Rules do no more than moderate, they prune the rampant vine, etc., etc. My dear friend, let me tell you what it is like. It is like love. A young man is heart and soul attached to a girl, spends every hour of the day with her, expends all his energies, all he owns, in demonstrating every minute that he is utterly hers. Then along comes a philistine, holder of some public office, and says to him, 'My dear young man, loving is human but you must love as a human being should. Divide up your hours, some for work, and those for recreation give to your girl. Calculate your assets, and having covered your needs by all means draw on what's left to make her a present now and then (only not too often), on her birthday or her name-day, for example.'—If the lover does as he's told he'll become a useful young man and I myself would recommend any prince to appoint him to one board or another. But that's the end of his love and, if he's an artist, of his art. My friends, I ask you, why does the river of genius so seldom burst its banks, so seldom surge high and roar upon you and shake and astonish your souls?—Friends, on both banks are the dwelling-places of placid gentlemen whose summer-houses, tulip beds, and vegetable plots would be destroyed and who therefore in good time ward off the future danger by damming and diverting.

27 May

I see that I have fallen into rhapsodies, likenesses, and declamation and have omitted to finish my story about the children. I must have sat two hours there on my plough deep in the painterly feelings I laid before you, very disjointedly, in my letter yesterday. Then near evening a young woman with a basket on her arm came striding towards the children, who in the meantime had not moved, and, still some way off, called out, 'You've been a good boy, Philip.'—She gave me good-day, I thanked her, stood up, approached her, and asked was she the mother of the children. 'Yes,' she said, and giving the elder boy half of a bread roll she took up the little one and kissed him very lovingly.—'I left Philip to look after the baby,' she said, 'and went into town with my eldest to buy white bread and sugar and a porridge pot.'—I could see all that in the basket, whose lid had come off.—'I'm going to make Hans' (so the youngest was called) 'some broth this evening. His rascal of a big brother broke my pot yesterday quarrelling with Philip over the scrapings of the porridge.'—I asked her about the eldest and she had scarcely told me that he was in the meadow chasing around with the geese when he came bounding on to the scene with a hazel wand for the second boy. I talked further with the woman and learned that she was the schoolmaster's daughter and that her husband had gone on a journey to Switzerland to claim a legacy left him by a cousin.—'They were trying to cheat him out of it,' she said, 'and didn't answer his letters, so he went himself. I hope nothing bad has happened to him, I haven't had any news.'—I found it hard leaving the woman, I gave each of the boys a penny and gave the mother one for the youngest also, to get him a bread roll to go with his broth when she next went to town, and so we parted.

My dear friend, I tell you, at times when I feel near to breaking, all the upheaval in me can be stilled by the sight of such a creature who, going her ways in happy serenity within the narrow circle of her existence, gets by from one day to the next and, seeing the leaves fall, thinks nothing other than that winter is coming.

I have often been out there since. The children are quite used to me, they get sugar when I drink my coffee and in the evening share my bread and curds. They never go without their pennies on a Sunday, and if I'm not there after vespers the landlady has instructions to pay the money out.

We are good friends, they tell me all manner of things, and I especially enjoy observing their passions and their innocent sudden cupidities when more children gather from the village.

I had hard work reassuring the mother that they weren't a nuisance to the gentleman.

30 May*

What I was saying recently about painting is certainly true of poetry too. We have only to recognize what is excellent and dare to speak it—which is asking a lot, I know. I witnessed an episode today which, simply written down, would make the loveliest idyll in the world. But what have poetry, episode, and idyll to do with it? Must a natural phenomenon always be worked up and improved before it will engage us?

If after this introduction you expect something lofty and superior then, not for the first time, you have been sorely deceived. I am rapt into this lively sympathy by nothing more than a farmhand. As usual, I shall tell it badly and, as usual, you will, I suspect, think me extravagant. And again it is Wahlheim, always Wahlheim, that brings forth these wonders.

There was a gathering of people under the lime trees, drinking coffee, and because they were not quite my sort I made an excuse and kept away.

A farmhand came out of a nearby house and busied himself

mending the plough I had sketched not long ago. His manner pleased me, I addressed him, asked after his circumstances, we were soon acquainted and, as usually happens to me with people of his kind, we were soon on friendly terms. He was, he told me, in service with a widow and she treated him very well. He said so many things about her and was so full of praise for her that I soon knew him to be devoted to her, body and soul. She was no longer young, he said, and had been badly treated by her first husband, did not wish to marry again, and it shone forth so clearly from his account how beautiful she was to him, how attractive, and how much he desired her to choose him so that he might expunge the memory of the wrongs of her first husband—but to make this person's pure affection, love, and loyalty palpable to you I should have to repeat everything he said, word for word. Indeed, I should need the gifts of the greatest poets truly to bring to life before you the expressiveness of his gestures, the music of his voice and the secret fire in his eyes. But really no words can convey the delicacy of feeling there present in all his being and demeanour. I should present him very crassly, whatever I said. I was especially moved by his fear that I might form an unfair opinion of his relationship with her and have doubts about the correctness of her behaviour. How appealing it was when he spoke of her figure, her body, that without the charms of youth powerfully attracted and bound him—I can repeat that only to myself in my innermost soul. Never in my life before have I seen urgency of desire and yearningly passionate need in such purity—indeed, I might say that in such purity I have never even conceived or dreamed it. Don't scold me if I tell you that the thought of this innocence and truthfulness burns in my soul and that the image of this fidelity and tenderness pursues me wherever I go, and that, as though I were myself on fire, I thirst and pine.

I shall now endeavour to see the woman herself as soon as possible—or, on second thoughts, I'll make sure I don't. It is better that I see her through the eyes of the man who loves her. Perhaps if I saw her with my own eyes she would not appear to me as she does now, and why should I spoil that beautiful image?

Why haven't I written to you?—You ask me that and yet you are a scholar. You ought to be able to guess that I am well, and indeed— In a word, I have made an acquaintance that has touched me more closely than any other here. I have—I don't know.

I shall find it hard to tell you in proper order how it came about that I have met a most lovable person. I am happy and full of delight, and so a poor narrator.

An angel! Bah! Every man has his angel, does he not? And yet I am not in a state to tell you in what ways she is perfect and why she is perfect, only that she has seized hold of all my thoughts and feelings.

So much simplicity with so much understanding, so much kindness with so much steadiness, and a quietness of soul with a life in truth and activity.—

But what blather that is, mere abstractions, by which not one touch of her real self is expressed. On another occasion—no, not on another occasion, I'll tell you now. If I don't do it now, I might never. Because, between you and me, since I began writing I have three times been on the point of laying down my pen, having my horse saddled, and riding out. And yet I vowed this morning that I wouldn't ride out, and every minute I go to the window to see how high the sun is still.— — —

I couldn't help myself, I had to go and see her. And here I am back again, Wilhelm, and I'll eat my supper and write to you. What bliss it is for my soul to see her in the midst of her eight adorable and lively brothers and sisters!—

But if I go on like this you'll be no wiser at the end than you were at the beginning. Listen then, I'll force myself to give you details.

I wrote to you recently that I had got to know S., the Land Steward, and that he had begged me to visit him soon in his hermitage—or rather in his own little kingdom. I neglected to do so and perhaps should never have gone had not chance disclosed to me the treasure that lies hidden in that quiet locality.

Our young people had organized a dance* in the country and

I was quite happy to attend. I offered my hand to a girl here who is good and beautiful but not otherwise important to me—and it was agreed that I should hire a carriage and drive out with my partner and her cousin to the place of the entertainment, picking up Charlotte S.* on the way.—'You will meet a beautiful young woman,' said my companion as we drove through the wide clearings to the hunting lodge.—'Beware you don't fall in love with her,' the cousin added.—'And why?' I asked.—'She is already taken,' she answered, 'by a very decent man who has gone off to put his affairs in order because his father has died, and to bid for a well-paid post.'—This information mattered little to me.

The sun was still a quarter of an hour above the mountains when we drew up at the yard gate. The weather was very sultry and the women expressed their anxieties about a thunderstorm that in small, heavy, greyish-white clouds seemed to be assembling along the horizon. Pretending to be weather-wise, I sought to allay their fears, but did myself suspect our entertainment might suffer a jolt.

I had got down and a maid, coming to the gate, begged our pardon, Mamselle Lotte wouldn't be a moment. I crossed the yard to the good solid house, and climbing the front steps and going in at the door I saw the most charming spectacle* I have ever seen. There in the hall six children, aged between eleven and two, were swarming around a girl of medium height and beautiful bearing in a simple white dress with pale red ribbons on the sleeves and bosom. She held a loaf of black bread and was cutting slices from it and giving them, according to age and appetite, to each of her little ones, with great affection. They, having for a long time reached up their hands till their evening bread was cut, in turn then uttered an artless 'Thank you,' content with it, and sprang aside or those of a quieter nature walked calmly off to the gate to view the strangers and the carriage in which their Lotte was to ride away.—'I'm sorry you have had to come in,' she said, 'and that I'm keeping the ladies waiting. What with getting dressed and making arrangements for the household in my absence I forgot to give the children their bread, and they won't have it cut by anyone but me.'—I paid her some small compliment, my soul rested entirely

on her form, her tone, her bearing, and I had just time enough to
recover from my surprise when she ran into the parlour to fetch
her gloves and her fan. The little ones watched me from a distance,
rather askance. I went up to the youngest, a joyously beautiful
child. He drew back—just as Lotte came through the door and
said, 'Louis, shake hands with our cousin.'—This the boy did,
quite unabashed, and I couldn't help kissing him warmly, despite
his runny little nose.—'Cousin?' I said, offering her my hand. 'Am
I so fortunate? Do you really think me worthy of being related to
you?'—'Oh,' she said with an easy smile, 'our family is very wide-
spread and I'd be surprised if you were the worst among them.'—
As we walked away she told Sophie, a girl of about eleven, the
oldest girl after herself, to take good care of the others and to give
her love to Papa when he came in from his ride. She told the
smaller ones they must obey their sister Sophie as they would herself, which some then expressly promised to do. But one saucy
little blonde of about six said, 'But she's not you, Lotte, we like
you best.'—The two oldest boys had climbed up behind in the
carriage and, at my intercession, she allowed them to ride with us
until we reached the trees, as long as they promised to hold on
tight and not squabble.

We had scarcely made ourselves comfortable and the young
women exchanged greetings and remarked upon one another's
dress, especially the hats, and with due comments gone through
the company we might expect at the dance, than Lotte halted the
carriage to let her brothers get down, whereupon each demanded
to kiss her hand again, which the eldest did with the affection and
gentleness natural to some fifteen-year-olds and the other with
much boisterous giddiness. She sent further love to the little ones
and we went on our way.

The cousin asked had she finished the book she had sent her
recently.—'No,' said Lotte, 'I don't like it, you can have it back.
The one before was no better either.'—I was astonished when I
asked what the books were and she told me:[1]—I found so much

---

[1] We have thought it necessary to suppress this part of the letter so as to give no one
any cause for complaint. Though really no author could care very much for the opinions
of a girl and an unsteady young man.

character in everything she said, I saw new charms, new facets of her spirit, shine forth from the features of her face at every word— and her face seemed to open in pleasure because in me she could feel herself understood.

'When I was younger,' she said, 'I loved novels more than anything. Heavens, how happy I was on a Sunday if I could find myself a corner and sink myself heart and soul in the good and bad fortunes of some Miss Jenny* or other. And I can't deny that such things still hold some charm for me. But since I so seldom come near a book, when I do it must be wholly to my taste. And I like those authors best in whom I rediscover my own world, whose experiences resemble mine, and whose stories are as interesting and touching to me as my own domestic life, which is of course not paradise but all in all and nevertheless a source of inexpressible happiness.'

I struggled to conceal how much these words moved me. Needless to say, I had little success: for when I heard her speak in passing of *The Vicar of Wakefield*,* of ——[1], I forgot myself completely and said everything that I was driven to say, and only after some time, when Lotte turned the conversation towards the others, did I notice that they had been sitting there all the while with wide-open eyes, really as though they were not there at all. The cousin more than once gave me an amused little look which I disregarded.

The talk turned to the enjoyment of dancing.—'The passion for it may be a fault,' said Lotte, 'but I willingly confess to you that I like nothing better than dancing. And when there's something bothering me, all's soon well again if I hammer out a country dance on my out-of-tune piano.'

How I feasted, while she spoke, on her black eyes; how the animation of her lips and the freshness and warmth of her cheeks pulled at my soul; how I, sunk deep in the sovereign *sense* of her speech, often did not hear the words with which she expressed it—knowing me, you will have some idea. In brief, when we halted

---

[1] Here also the names of one or two of our nation's authors have been omitted. Whoever enjoys Lotte's approval will surely feel it in his heart should he read this passage, and otherwise nobody needs to know.

at the dancing-place I got out of the carriage like a dreamer and was so lost in dreams in a world coming into being that I scarcely heeded the music coming down to us from the illuminated upper room.

We were met at the carriage door by the partners of the cousin and Lotte, a Mr Audran and another gentleman whose name I can't remember—who *can* remember all the names? They took possession of their ladies and I conducted mine upstairs.

We looped and threaded our way in minuets. I asked up one woman after another and it was always the least bearable of them who took longest to extend a farewell hand and make an end of it. Lotte and her partner began an *anglaise*,* and you will sense how glad I was when in her proceeding down the line she came to us. Oh, you should see her dancing! She is in it heart and soul, utterly, her whole body in harmony, so without care or inhibition, as though dancing were all there is and as though she had no other thought or feeling—and it is certain that in those moments all else vanishes from her view.

I asked her for the second *contre-danse*, she granted me the third and told me with the sweetest candour in the world that she passionately loved dancing the *allemande*.*—'It's the custom here', she went on, 'that all stay with their partners for the *allemande* and mine waltzes badly and would be grateful if I let him off. Your young lady is no good at it either and doesn't like it, and I noticed in the *anglaise* that you waltz very well. If you would like to be mine for the *allemande*, go and ask my gentleman if he minds and I'll go and ask your lady.'—We shook hands on it and arranged that her partner should entertain mine in the interim.

And off we went! And for a while enjoyed all manner of linkings and interlockings of the arms. How quick and charming she was in all her movements! And then when it came to the waltzing and the couples like planets orbiting one another, it was in fact, since very few had any skill at it, something of a chaos. Shrewdly we let them have their fling, and when the clumsiest had left the floor we made our entry and together with one other couple, Audran and his partner, stayed the course splendidly. I've never felt so light-footed. I was more than human. The sweet girl in my arms and whirling around with her like the stormwind till all about us lapsed away and—Wilhelm, in all honesty I must tell you I swore that, cost what it might, no girl I loved and had any claim on should ever waltz with anyone but me. You understand me, I'm sure.

We took a few turns about the room, walking now, to get our breath back. Then she sat down and the oranges, which I had put to one side and which were the only ones left, had just the desired effect except that whenever, as a matter of courtesy, she shared a piece with her rather forward neighbour, I felt a stab in the heart.

In the third *anglaise* we were the second couple. As we danced between the rows and I, with God knows what bliss, hung on her arm and gazed into her eyes in which the purest and frankest pleasure was expressed with all possible truth, we came to a woman whose sweet looks in a face no longer young I had already noticed and thought remarkable. She looked at Lotte with a smile, raised a warning finger, and twice, as we flew past, uttered the name Albert in very meaningful tones.

'Who is Albert?' I said to Lotte, 'if I may make so bold as to ask.'—She was about to answer when we were obliged to separate for the grand figure of eight, and I seemed to see a slight pondering on her brows when we passed one another crossing over.— 'Why should I hide it from you?' she said, giving me her hand for the promenade. 'Albert is an excellent man to whom I am as good as engaged.'—Now, this was nothing new to me (the girls had told me on the way) and yet it was wholly new since I had not yet considered it in relation to her who in so short a time had grown so important to me. In brief, I became confused, forgot what I was doing, and got in between the wrong couple so that everything was at sixes and sevens and it took all Lotte's presence of mind and tugging and towing to bring us smartly back into order.

The dance was not yet at an end when the lightning, that we had for a long time seen flashing on the horizon and that I had insisted was only the cooling of the atmosphere, began to be much stronger and the thunder outdid the music. Three young women ran from the lines and their gentlemen followed them; disorder became general and the music ceased. It is natural that if some fright or calamity surprises us when we are enjoying ourselves it will affect us more strongly than usual, in part because of the contrast thus made very palpable, and in part, and perhaps more, because our senses have been opened to feeling and so take in impressions faster. These are the reasons I must adduce to explain the wondrous antics several of the young women now fell to performing. The most sensible of them sat herself down in a corner with her back to the window and covered her ears. A second knelt and buried her head in the seated woman's lap. A third pushed in between and clung to both her young companions in floods of tears. Some wanted to go home; others, yet more at a loss, were not even *compos mentis* enough to curb the impudence of certain youths whose chief concern, as it seemed, was to snatch the anxious prayers intended for heaven from the very lips of beauty in distress. Some of our gentlemen had gone downstairs to smoke their pipes in peace, and the rest of the company gladly accepted the landlady's sensible offer of a room that had shutters and curtains. As soon as we were there, Lotte busied herself putting chairs in a circle, and having asked everyone to be seated she prepared us for a game.

I saw more than one young man pursing up his lips and stretching himself in the hope of some juicy forfeit.—'We'll play counting,' she said. 'Now pay attention. I go round the circle from right to left and you count anti-clockwise too, each saying the number that comes to you and we must go like the wind and anyone who hesitates or makes a mistake gets a slap and so on to a thousand.'— What a comical spectacle it was! She went round the circle with her arm outstretched. 'One,' said the first, 'two,' the next, 'three,' the next, and so on. Then she began to go faster, and faster still. Came the first mistake—and slap! And in all the jeering and laughter the next in turn got a slap also. And so on, faster and faster. I got my ear clipped twice and with deep satisfaction thought I noticed that the blows were harder than those she was dealing the rest of the company. The game ended in general merriment and tumult before we reached the thousand. Couples wanting no one but themselves drew aside, the thunderstorm was over, and I followed Lotte back into the big room. On the way there she said, 'Having their ears boxed made them forget thunder and lightning and everything else.'—I could think of nothing to say to her in reply.—'Myself,' she continued, 'I was one of the most fearful, but pretending to be brave, to encourage the others, I became courageous too.'—We went to the window. There was still thunder away to one side, the rain fell in a glorious rushing on the land, and scents rose, in quickening abundance, on warm airs to us. She stood leaning on her elbows, her gaze went deep into everything around, she looked up at the heavens, then at me, and I saw that her eyes were full of tears, she laid her hand on mine and said, 'Klopstock!'—At once I remembered the wonderful ode* she had in mind and I sank in the flood of feelings that by this watchword she had unleashed in me. I could not bear it, I bowed and kissed her hand in an ecstasy of tearful joy. And looked again into her eyes.—Ah Klopstock, had you seen the adoration of you in those eyes! And now may I never hear your name, so often profaned, from any lips but hers.

19 June

I don't know how far I got in my story last time but I do know it was two in the morning before I went to bed and that if I'd been able to tell it you face to face instead of writing it I should perhaps have kept you up till dawn.

I still haven't told you what happened on our drive back from the dance, and today isn't the day for it either.

Sunrise was splendid. The trees still dripping and the quickened fields all around! The young women with us fell asleep. She asked me if I'd like to do the same and said not to mind about her.—'No danger of that,' I said, gazing at her, 'so long as I see those eyes of yours open.'—And we both held out till her door, where the maid quietly let her in and answered, when she asked, that Father and the little ones were all well and were still sleeping. I left her—but not before asking whether I might see her again that same day, which she agreed to, and I did, and since that time sun and moon and stars can all go about their business as they please, I don't know whether it's day or night and the whole world is lapsing from my view.

21 June

I live such days of happiness as God saves for his saints, and whatever happens to me I could never say that the joys, the purest joys, of life have been denied me.—I've told you about my Wahlheim, I am fully established there now, from there it is only half an hour to Lotte, there I feel my own life and all the happiness ever given to a human being.

Little did I think when I chose Wahlheim for the object of my walks that it lay so near to heaven! How often on my extended wanderings I have noticed the hunting lodge, now the repository of all my desires, either from the hills or from the valley floor, across the river.

My dear Wilhelm, I've had all manner of thoughts about the desire human beings have to extend themselves, to make new discoveries, to rove far and wide; and then about the impulse in them willingly to accept constraints and to proceed along the track of habit untroubled by what might be to the left or right of it.

Strange and wonderful, how I came here and looked from the hill down into the lovely valley and how drawn I was then in every direction.—The wood there!—Oh to mix with its shadows!—That mountain-top!—Oh to survey the whole wide country from up there!—And the hills linked one into another and the secret valleys between!—Oh to lose myself in them!—I set off in haste and returned and had not found what I hoped for. Oh, distances are like the future! A vast dawning entirety lies before the soul, our senses lose themselves in it as do our eyes and oh! we long to make the oblation of all our being and to be filled utterly with the bliss of a single large and glorious feeling.—And oh! when we hurry after it, when There becomes Here, all is as it was and we stand in our poverty, in our narrowness, and the soul in us parches for the elusive freshening.

So the most restless wanderer longs in the end for his homeland again and finds in his cottage, in the arms of his wife, in the midst of his children, in the work of looking after them, the joy he had sought in vain in the wide world.

When at sunrise every morning I walk out to my Wahlheim and

there in the landlady's garden pick my own sugar peas, sit down and trim them, reading in my Homer the while; and then in the little kitchen choose a pan, take a knob of butter, put the peas on the flame, cover them, sit by to stir them now and then: I have such a lively sense of how the suitors* in their insolence slaughtered, jointed, and roasted Penelope's swine and cattle. Nothing fills me more completely with warm and true feelings than do such details of patriarchal life which I, thank God, can weave without any affectation into my own way of living.

How glad I am that my heart can feel the simple and harmless joy of the man who brings a cabbage to his table that he grew himself and enjoys as he eats it the morning he planted it, the evenings he watered it, the delight he had in its thriving and growth, all that, all those good days, as he eats, he enjoys them again.

29 June

The day before yesterday the Doctor came out here from the town to see the Land Steward and found me on the ground under Lotte's children, some climbing around on top of me, others attacking me, whilst I tickled them and all of us together made a great noise. The Doctor, a very pedantic marionette, always straightening his sleeves as he talks and showing off volumes of fancy cuffs, thought all this beneath the dignity of any man of sense, as was obvious from the face he pulled. I heeded him not at all, let him transact his very sensible business, and built the children their houses of cards again, which they had demolished. And he went about town afterwards lamenting that the Land Steward's children, ill brought up already, were now being ruined utterly by Werther.

Yes, my dear Wilhelm, of all earthly creatures children are closest to my heart. When I watch them and see in their small forms the seeds of all the strengths and virtues that one day they will have such need of; when I perceive in their obstinacy a future resilience and firmness of character, and in their mischief the good humour and lightness that will help them slip through the dangers of the world, and all so unspoilt and whole, then over and over again I recall the golden words of the Teacher of Mankind: unless ye become as one of these.* And yet, my dear friend, these our equals, who should be our models, do we not treat them as our inferiors? They shan't have minds of their own!—But don't *we*? And what gives us that privilege?—Our being older and wiser!—All God sees from His heaven are children, some old, some young, and His son told us long ago which He has more joy in. But they believe in Him and don't listen to Him—that's an old story too—and bring up their children in their own image and—adieu, Wilhelm! I've no wish to harp on about it any longer.

1 July

What Lotte must be to the sick I can feel in my own poor heart that is worse off than many a one languishing ill in bed. She is to spend a few days in the town with an estimable woman who, according to the doctors, is nearing her end and who in these last moments wants Lotte near her. Last week she and I went to visit the Pastor in St., which is a tiny place off the beaten track an hour away in the hills. We got there about four. Lotte had brought her second sister along. When we reached the parsonage, whose forecourt is shaded by two tall walnut trees, the amiable old man was sitting on a bench by the front door. The sight of Lotte seemed to give him new life, he forgot his gnarled walking-stick and ventured forward to greet her. She ran towards him, insisted he sit down again, sat next to him, passed on her father's warmest good wishes, and hugged the Pastor's youngest son, a dirty and unattractive child, the darling of his old age. You should have seen how she engaged the old man, how she raised her voice to be heard by his half-deaf ears, told him of robust young people suddenly dying, said how excellent the waters of Karlsbad* were, commended his decision to go there next summer, and told him that he looked much better, and was much more sprightly, than when she saw him last.—In the meantime I had been paying my compliments to the Pastor's wife. The old man became very cheerful, and when I said how much I admired the beautiful walnuts shading us so agreeably, he began, not without some difficulty, to tell us their story.—'The older tree,' he said, 'we don't know who planted it: some say one pastor, some another. But the younger tree at the back there is as old as my wife, fifty years in October. Her father planted it in the morning and she was born that same day, towards evening. He was my predecessor in office. He loved the tree more than can be said and certainly I love it no less. My wife was sitting under it on a block of wood, knitting, twenty-seven years ago when I first came in here as a poor student.'—Lotte asked after his daughter: she had gone out to the meadows, to the workers, with Herr Schmidt, apparently. And the old man went on with his story: how his predecessor had taken a liking to him, as had the daughter also, and how he had first become his assistant, then his successor. He had barely finished the tale when the girl, his own daughter, came through the garden with the man they had called Herr Schmidt. She welcomed Lotte in a very heartfelt manner, and I must say I did not at all dislike her—a quick and shapely brunette with whom one might have whiled away the rural hours very pleasantly. Her admirer (for as such Herr Schmidt at once presented himself) was a refined but taciturn man who would not take part in our conversation despite Lotte's continual efforts to include him. What bothered me most was that I seemed to see in his face it was more obduracy and bad humour than any narrowness of intellect which prevented him from communicating. Subsequently, alas, this became all too obvious; for on our walk, whenever Friederike* walked with Lotte, and now and then with me, the gentleman's complexion, already quite dark, got visibly so much darker that Lotte thought it time to tug me by the sleeve and warn me that I had been rather too gallant with Friederike. Now, nothing annoys me more than when people torment one another, especially when young people who, in the bloom of life, could be at their most open to all manner of delights, spoil the few good days for one another by a sour behaviour and realize only when it is too late to make good, just what they have wasted. This continued to irk me, and when towards evening we returned to the parsonage and were sitting at the table eating curds and the conversation turned to the joys and sorrows of the world, I couldn't help taking up the subject again and speaking out with some passion against bad moods.—'People are forever complaining', I began, 'that good days are few and bad days many, and they do so, it seems to me, for the most part unjustly. If we always kept our hearts open to enjoy the good that God prepares for us daily we should then have the strength to bear the ills when they come.'—'But it is not in our power to control our spirits,' the Pastor's wife answered. 'So much depends on our bodies. If we don't feel well, nothing at all is right.'—I granted her that.—'Then,' I continued, 'let us view it as a sickness and ask is there any remedy.'—'Indeed yes,' said Lotte. 'I for one believe much depends on ourselves. I know it from my own experience. If something nags at me and is making me cross I jump up and sing a few country-dance tunes up and down the garden, and that soon gets rid of it.'—'That is what I meant,' I said. 'Bad moods are just like sloth, indeed they are a form of sloth. Both are very natural to us, but if we only have the strength to pull ourselves together the task becomes easy and in being active we can find a real pleasure.'—Friederike was paying close attention. Her young man objected that one wasn't master of oneself. Least of all could we command our feelings.—'Here it is a question of an unpleasant feeling,' I replied, 'that surely any person would be glad to be rid of. And no one knows how far his strength might reach till he has tried it. We know for certain that a person who is ill will seek advice from all the doctors and will accept the greatest sacrifices or the bitterest medicines to regain the good health he desires.'—I noticed that the honest old gentleman was straining his hearing to take part in our discussion and I raised my voice and turned to him. 'There are sermons against so many vices,' I said, 'but I have never heard that the pulpit has been used to combat bad moods.'[1]—'That's something for the preachers in the towns,' he said. 'Country-people are never in an ill humour. But sometimes it wouldn't hurt. It would serve as a homily for one's wife, at least, and for the Land Steward.'—We all laughed, and so did he, very heartily, until he fell into a coughing which interrupted our discussion for a while. Then the young man resumed it: 'You called ill humour a vice. That seems to me an

---

[1] We do now have an excellent sermon by Lavater* on this subject, among those on the Book of Jonah.

exaggeration.'—'Not at all,' I answered, 'if a thing that harms myself and my neighbour deserves that name. Is it not enough that we cannot make one another happy, must we also rob one another of the pleasures that any heart may permit itself now and then? And name me a person who in a bad mood will be decent enough to hide it, to bear it alone, without destroying the joy around him. Is it not rather an inner dissatisfaction with our own unworthiness, a dislike of ourselves that is always associated with envy aggravated by foolish conceit? We see people happy and not made happy by us, and that is unbearable.'—Lotte smiled at me, seeing how what I was saying wrought me up, and tears in Friederike's eyes spurred me on.—'No credit to those,' I said, 'who use the power they have over a heart to rob it of the simple joys that are engendered in it. No gifts and courtesies of the world can make up for that moment's pleasure in ourselves spoilt for us by the envious truculence of our tyrant.'

My whole heart was full at this moment; the memory of many a past thing pressed at my soul and tears came to my eyes.

'We should remind ourselves daily,' I cried: 'all you can do for your friends is allow them their pleasures and increase their happiness by sharing it. For when their souls are tormented by some unnerving passion or battered by sorrow, is it in your power to give them one drop of relief?

'And when the last and most fearful sickness falls upon a person whom in her heyday you undermined and she lies there now in pitiable exhaustion, her eyes turned unfeelingly to heaven, the sweats of death ever present on her brow, and you stand by her bed like one of the damned and know in your innermost heart that all your powers are powerless and you writhe in the agony of wishing that into this failing creature by some total sacrifice you could instil one drop that would strengthen her, one spark that would give her courage—'

The memory of such a scene, at which I had been present, came over me with full violence at these words. I covered my eyes with a handkerchief and left the company and only Lotte's calling we should go restored me to myself. And how on the way back she scolded me for my too passionate sympathies in everything and

that it would be the end of me, that I should spare myself.—Oh
the angel! For your sake I must live.

6 July

She is still with her dying friend, and always the same, always the
sweet and present creature who, wherever she looks, soothes pain
and makes people happy. Yesterday evening she went for a walk
with Marianna and little Malchen,* I knew and I found her and we
all went together. After walking for an hour and a half we came
back towards the town, to the well already dear to me and now a
thousand times dearer. Lotte sat down on the low wall, we stood
before her. I looked around and oh, the days when my heart was
so alone revived in me.—And I said, 'Such a beloved place, and
yet since those days I have never rested in its coolness and sometimes have hurried by without a look.'—I glanced down and saw
that Malchen in a very busy fashion was climbing up with a glass
of water.—I looked at Lotte and felt all that she means to me.
Malchen meanwhile arrived with the glass. Marianna wanted to
take it from her. 'No,' the child cried, with the sweetest expression, 'no, Lottchen, you must drink first.'—I was so ravished by
the truth and goodness of her exclamation that my feelings could
only be expressed by lifting the child up and kissing her warmly—
whereupon she at once began to scream and cry.—'You shouldn't
have done that,' said Lotte.—I was taken aback.—'Come,
Malchen,' she continued, taking her by the hand and leading her
down the steps, 'wash yourself with the fresh spring water, quickly,
quickly, and no harm's done.'—And I stood there and watched
how busily the little girl rubbed at her cheeks with her wet hands
in the firm belief that all defilement would be washed clean and
she would be saved from the shame of getting a horrible beard,
and when Lotte said, 'That will do,' and the child carried on energetically washing herself, to make sure and doubly sure—I tell
you, Wilhelm, I've never felt more respectful at a christening—
and when Lotte came up I'd have liked to prostrate myself before
her as before a prophet who had by holy rituals taken away the sins
of a nation.

That evening in the joy of my heart I couldn't help relating the occurrence to a man I knew to be intelligent and whom, for that reason, I credited with some human understanding. I was very mistaken! He said it was quite wrong of Lotte, children shouldn't be deceived, it led to countless errors and superstitions against which they should be protected from the start.—Then I remembered that a week before this man had had a child baptized, so I let it go and remained faithful to the truth in my heart. We should treat children as God treats us, and He makes us happiest when He lets us totter along in benign illusions.

8 July

What children we are! How we hunger for a certain look! What children we are!—We had gone out to Wahlheim. The women drove there. Then in the course of our walks I thought that in Lotte's black eyes—I'm a fool, forgive me, you ought to see those eyes.—I'll be brief (my eyes are falling shut with sleep), the women got back in and standing around the carriage were young W., Selstadt, Audran, and myself. Through the carriage window then there was some chatter with these boys who were, needless to say, as airy and light-hearted as you could wish.—I sought Lotte's eyes. Oh, they passed from one to the next, but me, me, me, who stood there waiting and hoping for nothing else, they never looked at me!—My heart was bidding her a thousand goodbyes and she didn't see me. The carriage moved off and there were tears in my eyes. I watched it drawing away and I saw Lotte's hat as she leaned out and as she turned to look—oh, for me?—My dear friend, I am still uncertain. It is a comfort to me, perhaps she was looking back for me! Perhaps.—Good-night. Oh what a child I am!

10 July

You should see how foolish I look in company when there's any mention of her. And if someone actually asks me do I like her!— Like! I hate the word with a passion. What kind of person must he be who *likes* Lotte, whose every sense and feeling is not utterly

possessed by her. Like! Not long ago someone asked me did I like
Ossian!*

Frau M. is very poorly. I pray for her life because I feel for her
with Lotte. I see Lotte rarely, at the house of one of her friends,
and today she told me an extraordinary story.—M. is a grasping
old skinflint who has given his wife much trouble and greatly
restricted her life; but she has always managed to get by. A few
days ago, when the doctor told her there was no hope, she summoned this husband (Lotte was in the room) and said to him: 'I
have to confess something which might cause confusion and
annoyance after my death. I have until now kept house with as
much order and thrift as I could but—forgive me—during these
thirty years I have been deceiving you. At the start of our marriage
you fixed a small sum of money for the kitchen and other household expenses. When our household grew and our business was
larger you could not be persuaded to increase my weekly allowance
according to our changing circumstances. In brief, as you know,
when our outgoings were at their greatest you still insisted I must
manage on seven gulden a week. I accepted that sum without argument and every week took the extra out of our takings, since
nobody would suspect the woman of the house might rob the till.
I never spent more than was necessary, and even without confessing it I should have gone to meet my Maker with a clear conscience. But whoever has to keep house after me would not know
how to manage and you would be able to insist that your first wife
got by on that amount.'

I marvelled with Lotte at the man's incredible blindness of mind
who does not suspect there is something amiss when his wife still
manages on seven gulden a week though, as he must see, the
expenses have perhaps doubled. But I've known people myself
who would believe they had the prophet's unfailing cruse of oil* in
their house and never wonder about it.

13 July

No, I am not deceiving myself. In her black eyes I read a real sympathy for me and for my fate. Indeed, I feel, and trust my heart in this, that she—oh, am I permitted to utter the heaven that is in these words?—that she loves me.

Loves me!—And how I value myself, how—I can surely say this to you, you understand such things—how I adore myself now that she loves me.*

Is that hubris or a feeling of how things truly are?—I don't know anyone from whom I have anything to fear in Lotte's heart. And yet—when she speaks of the man she is engaged to, speaks of him with such warmth, such love—then I'm like a man stripped of all honour and status and whose sword has been taken from him.

16 July

Oh how it courses all through my veins when by accident my finger touches hers or when our feet touch under the table. I pull back as though from fire and a mysterious force draws me on again—there is a fainting in all my senses.—And oh, in her innocence, in her uninhibited soul, she does not feel how these small intimacies torment me. And when we are talking and she puts her hand on mine and for the ease of conversation moves nearer to me so that the heavenly breath of her mouth can reach my lips:—I seem to lapse away as though touched by lightning.—And Wilhelm, if I ever dared—if by me this heaven, this trust—You understand me. No, my heart is not so depraved. Weak, weak enough!—And is that not a depravity?—

She is sacred to me. All desire falls silent in her presence. I can never say what it is like when I am with her, it's as if in every nerve my soul was turned about.—There is a tune she plays on the piano with the force of any angel, so simple and so full of the spirit. It is her favourite song and it recovers me from every pain, confusion, and foolishness as soon as she strikes the first note.

Nothing ever said about music's ancient magical power seems improbable to me. How that simple song seizes hold of me! And how well she knows when to play it, often at a time when I'd like to put a bullet through my head. The error and darkness in my soul are dispersed and I breathe freely again.

18 July

Wilhelm what is our world like without love? Like a magic lantern without a light. The moment you bring the little lamp into it, the brightest pictures shine on your white wall. And if it were no more than that, only passing phantoms, still it always makes us happy when we stand there like innocent boys enraptured by the wondrous visions. I couldn't visit Lotte today, an unavoidable social engagement prevented me. What should I do? I sent my servant, just to have someone around me who had seen her. How impatiently I awaited him, how glad I was to see him again. I'd have taken his head between my hands and kissed him, but for the shame.

We are told that if you lay Bologna stone* in the sun it will absorb the rays and will shine for a while in the night. My young man was the same. The feeling that her eyes had rested on his face, his cheeks, the buttons of his jacket, the collar of his outdoor coat, made them all so holy and precious to me, and at that moment I wouldn't have parted with him for a thousand thalers. I felt such happiness in his presence.—God forbid that you should laugh at me. Are they phantoms, Wilhelm, if they make us happy?

19 July

'I shall see her,' I say aloud in the morning when I wake and with all cheerfulness look towards the lovely sun, 'I shall see her!' And for the whole day then I have no further wish. Everything, everything is consumed in this one prospect.

20 July

I can't yet share your view that I should travel with the Envoy* to ——. I am no great friend of rank and on top of that, as we all know, he is a repellent person. You say my mother would be glad to see me occupied. That made me laugh. Am I not occupied now? And in fact is it not all one whether I count peas or lentils? It's all a nonsense, and a man who at the behest of other people and not for his own passion or need works himself into the ground, for money or status or whatever else, is always a fool.

24 July

Since you are so concerned that I shouldn't neglect my drawing I'd rather pass over the whole subject in silence than tell you that for some time now I have done very little.

I've never been so happy, never was my feeling for nature, down to the smallest stone or blade of grass, so full and heartfelt, and yet—I don't know how to express myself, my powers of representation are so weak, everything drifts and wavers so before my soul, I can't grasp hold of any outline. But I tell myself that if I had clay or wax I could very well shape something. And I will get some clay if this lasts much longer and knead it even if all I make is cakes!

Three times I've begun Lotte's portrait and three times the result was a disgrace. I am all the more aggrieved by this since a while ago I was very lucky in my likenesses. Now I have done a silhouette of her and I'll have to be content with that.

To Lotte   *26 July**

Yes, my dear Lotte, I'll see to it, I'll order what you want. Do give me more commissions, many and often. Only one thing I ask: please don't sprinkle sand on the little notes you write. I pressed today's quickly to my lips and my teeth grated.

To Wilhelm   *26 July*

I have sometimes resolved not to see her so often. But who could keep to that? Every day I give in to the temptation, and swear again by all that's holy: tomorrow you will stay away for once. And when morning comes, again I discover some utterly compelling

reason and before I know it I am with her. Either the previous
evening she said, 'You'll come tomorrow, won't you?'—Then who
could stay away? Or she gives me some commission and I find it
best to tell her the outcome myself. Or the day is just too beautiful,
I walk out to Wahlheim and once I'm there it is only half an hour
further to her—I am already in her atmosphere, too close—
Whoosh! I'm there! My grandmother used to tell a fairy story
about the Magnetic Mountain:* ships that came too close were
suddenly robbed of all their iron, the nails flew off to the mountain
and the poor wretches foundered among the disassembling
planks.

30 July

Albert has come and I shall leave. And even were he the best and
noblest of men, whom I should be willing to acknowledge my
superior in every respect, still it would be unbearable to have him
before my eyes in the possession of all the perfections she
embodies.—Possession!—Enough, Wilhelm, her betrothed has
come, a decent and lovable man, impossible to wish him ill.
Fortunately I was not there when he arrived. It would have ripped
my heart to shreds. And he is so honourable and has not once
kissed Lotte in my presence. God reward him for that. I am bound
to love him for the respect he shows the girl. He wishes me well,
which I suppose to be Lotte's doing more than a work of his own
feelings. Women are subtle in things of that sort, and rightly. If she
can keep two admirers on good terms with one another—not many
could!—it will always be to her advantage.

And I can't deny Albert my esteem. His equable demeanour
contrasts very sharply with the always obvious restlessness of my
own character. He is a man of deep feeling and knows what he
has in Lotte. He seems scarcely ever to be in a bad mood, and
bad moods are, as you know, the sin I detest above all others in
people.

He thinks me a man of sense, and my devotion to Lotte, the
warm delight I take in all she does, increases his triumph and he
loves her all the more. Whether he doesn't sometimes torment her

with little fits of jealousy, who knows? Myself, were I in his position, I should not be entirely safe from that devil, I am sure.

But all that is neither here nor there. My joy in being with Lotte is over. Shall I call it folly or blindness?—Why give it any name?—The thing speaks for itself.—I knew everything I know now before Albert came. I knew I could have no claim on her and I never made any—at least, in so far as it is possible not to desire what is so lovable—And how amazed the fool looks when the other man does indeed turn up and takes the girl from him!

I clench my teeth and laugh at my misery, but double and treble I laugh at those who would tell me I must resign myself, for how else could it end?—Spare me their twaddle!—I wander around in the woods, and when I come to Lotte and Albert is sitting in the little garden with her in the arbour and it is too much for me, then I run wild in foolishness and start up in all manner of extravagance and nonsense.—'For heaven's sake,' Lotte said to me today, 'no more scenes like yesterday evening, please. You are frightful when you play the fool like that.'—Between you and me, I wait for times when he is busy and then in a trice I'm there and all is well with me when I find her alone.

8 August

Believe me, my dear Wilhelm, I certainly didn't have you in mind when I said I couldn't bear people who insist we should accept the inevitable. It really did not occur to me that you might incline to that opinion. And when all's said and done, you are right. Only one thing, my dear friend: Either–Or is rarely an adequate formula for life. There are as many gradations in feelings and ways of behaving as there are between a snub nose and an aquiline.

You won't take it amiss then if I concede your entire argument and try nevertheless to wriggle between the Either and the Or.

Either, you say, you have some hopes of Lotte or you have none. Good. If the former, seek to carry them through, seek to accomplish your desires. If the latter, pull yourself together and seek to be rid of a miserable emotion which is bound in the end to consume all your energies. My dear friend, that is well said—and sooner said than done.

And can you demand of a wretch whose life is being gradually and inexorably sapped by a wasting illness, can you demand that he puts a sudden end to the torment with the thrust of a dagger? Does not the very malady consuming his energies rob him also of the courage to free himself of it?

True, you could answer me with a kindred analogy. Who wouldn't rather have his arm taken off than by dithering and cowardice put his life at risk?—I don't know.—And let us not worry at one another with analogies. Wilhelm, I do indeed have moments of enough courage to leap up, shake myself free, and go—if I knew where.

Evening*

I came across my diary again today, which for some time I have neglected, and I'm astonished how consciously, step by step, I walked into it all. How clearly I have always seen my condition and acted like a child nevertheless, and how clearly I still see now, and still with no sign of a cure.

10 August

I could have the best and happiest life if I weren't a fool. Rarely do beautiful circumstances combine to delight the human soul as these have in which I find myself. Oh for sure, the heart is the maker of its own happiness!—To be a member of this lovable family, to be loved by the old widower like a son, by the children like a father, and by Lotte!—And then Albert, the honest man, who never spoils my happiness with any moodiness or incivility; who embraces me in heartfelt friendship and to whom, after Lotte, I am the dearest person in the world.—Wilhelm, it is a joy to hear us on our walks talking about Lotte: nothing on earth was ever dreamed up more ridiculous than this relationship, and yet often I have tears in my eyes over it.

When he tells me about her admirable mother: how on her

deathbed she entrusted her household and her children to Lotte and commended Lotte to him; how from that day forth a wholly different spirit animated Lotte; how she, in her careful management, in her seriousness, had become a true mother; how not one minute of her time went by without active love and work, and yet in it her cheerfulness and lightness of heart never deserted her.— And I walk beside him and pick flowers along the way, with great care make a bouquet of them and—fling them into the river flowing by and watch them travel quietly downstream.—I don't know whether I told you that Albert will stay here, and at the Court, where he is very well liked, he will have a post and a good salary. I have seen few to equal him for order and diligence in managing things.

12 August

Without a doubt, there's no better person than Albert under the sun. I had a strange scene with him yesterday. I came to say goodbye, having suddenly felt like riding into the mountains, from where indeed I am now writing to you, and as I was pacing up and down in the room I caught sight of his pistols.—'Lend me your pistols, will you,' I said, 'for my journey.'—'Gladly,' he said, 'if you can be bothered to load them. I only hang them there for show.'—I took one of them down and he continued: 'Precautions got me into such trouble once that I've wanted nothing to do with pistols since.'—I was curious to hear the story.—'For three months or more,' he said, 'I had been living in the country with a friend, kept a pair of pistols by me, unloaded, and slept easy. Then one rainy afternoon I was sitting there doing nothing and, I don't know why, it occurred to me that we might be attacked, might need the pistols, and might—you know how it is.—I gave them to the servant to clean and load, he was playing around, to frighten the girls, and, God knows how, the gun went off with the ramrod still in it and one of the girls got the rod in the ball of her right hand and it smashed her thumb. I had the whole fuss, and the costs of her treatment to pay as well, and since then I've never loaded my weapons. So much for taking precautions, my friend! There'll always be some risk you hadn't thought of. Admittedly . . .'—Now, as you know, I am very fond of the man until he comes to his 'admittedly'. For is it not obvious that every general statement must have its exceptions? But he is such a scrupulous person that if ever he thinks he has said something hasty, too general, only half-true, he must go on circumscribing, modifying, adding and subtracting till in the end there's nothing of the original statement left. On this occasion he worked his text very thoroughly, I stopped listening, I began to fool around, and in a sudden movement pressed the pistol against my forehead, above the right eye.— 'What on earth are you doing?' said Albert, pulling the weapon down.—'It's not loaded,' I said.—'Even so,' he answered impatiently. 'I can't imagine how anyone could be so foolish as to shoot himself. The very thought disgusts me.'

'Why must people,' I cried, 'when they speak of a thing say at once this is foolish, this is wise, this is good, this is bad? And what does it all mean when they do? Have they first delved into the inner circumstances of an act? Can they with certainty unravel the reasons why it was done, why it was bound to be done? If they have and can, surely they would not be so quick to judge.'

'You will concede', said Albert, 'that certain acts are wrong whatever their motivation.'

I shrugged and conceded it.—'But my dear Albert,' I continued, 'even here there are some exceptions. True, stealing is wrong: but a man who goes stealing to save himself and his family from present starvation, does he deserve punishment or sympathy? Who will cast the first stone* at the husband who in righteous anger slays his faithless wife and her vile seducer? Or at the girl who in one blissful hour gives herself up to the overwhelming joys of love? Even our laws, cold-blooded pedants though they are, allow themselves to be moved and hold back their punishment.'

'That is quite another matter,' Albert replied. 'For a man carried away by his passions loses all power of reflection and is viewed as drunk or mad.'

'You people and your reasonableness!' I exclaimed with a smile. 'And the passionate, the drunk, the mad—you stand there so calmly, so without sympathy, you with your morals, scold the drinker, abominate the madman, pass by like the priest, and thank God like the Pharisee* that he has not made you like one of these. I have been drunk more than once, my passions were never far from madness, and I regret neither for I have understood in my own capacity that all extraordinary people who ever achieved anything great, anything that seemed impossible, were always certain to be vilified as drunks and lunatics.

'But in ordinary life also it is intolerable to hear it said of almost anyone doing anything even half-ways free, noble, unexpected, The man is drunk! The man's a fool! Shame on you all in your sobriety and your wisdom!'

'Far-fetched again!' said Albert. 'You exaggerate everything, and here at least you are quite wrong in comparing suicide, which is what we are talking about, with great deeds. For really it can't be thought anything but a weakness. Of course it is easier to die than to bear a life of torment with fortitude.'

I was about to break off; for nothing upsets me more in an argument than to have someone come at me with a trivial commonplace when I have been speaking from the bottom of my heart. But I controlled myself because I have heard the like often before and have often been angered by it. I answered him with some force: 'You call that weakness? I beg you, don't be misled by appearances. A people groaning under the unbearable oppression of a tyrant, can you call it weakness when they finally rise up and break their chains? A man whose house has caught fire and who in terror feels a tensing of all his strength and with ease carries away burdens that in a quiet state he could scarcely move; or one who, infuriated by some insult, takes on and overcomes six opponents; are they to be called weak? And if such exertion, my dear friend, is a strength why should an extreme degree of it be a weakness?'—Albert looked at me and said, 'Don't be offended, but the examples you give do not seem at all apt.'—'That may be,' I said. 'I've often been told that the way I put things verges at times on nonsense. So let us see if there's another way of imagining what a person must feel like who decides to shuffle off the normally agreeable burden of being alive. For it isn't right that we should speak about things we cannot sympathize with.

'Human nature', I continued, 'has its limits. It can bear joy, sorrow, pain to a certain degree and founders when that limit is exceeded. So it is not a question of whether a person is weak or strong but of whether he can withstand the measure of his sufferings, be they physical, mental, or emotional. And I find it as strange to call a man a coward for taking his own life as it would be improper to call him cowardly for dying of a malignant fever.'

'False logic!' Albert cried.—'Not as false as you think,' I answered. 'You will concede that when a sickness attacks the constitution and so consumes or impairs its energies that it can't reverse the process, can't lift itself again and restore life to its usual happy course, we say this is a sickness unto death.*

'Now, my friend, let us apply that to the mind. Consider the person in his limitations, how impressions work upon him, ideas take hold of him, until in the end some growing passion robs him of all tranquil power of thought and drives him to destruction.

'Quite vainly will a placid and reasonable man contemplate and address this unhappy person's condition. Just as a healthy man standing at a sickbed can impart nothing whatsoever of his own vital forces to the invalid.'

Albert thought this all too general. I reminded him of a girl who only recently had been found drowned,* and I told him her story again.—An innocent young thing who had grown up in the narrow circle of domestic occupations and the week's prescribed labour, who had no other prospect of enjoyment than perhaps on Sundays to go walking in the town with others of her kind in whatever finery she had bit by bit assembled, perhaps now and then on high days and holidays to go dancing and apart from that to have a lively and heartfelt gossip with a neighbour for an hour or so about some quarrel or calumny.—Now finally her passionate nature begins to feel deeper needs, which are then increased by the flattering attentions she has from men. Her former pleasures gradually lose their savour, until at last she lights upon one man and by feelings she has never known before she is carried irresistibly to him, casts all her hopes on him, forgets the rest of the world, hears nothing, sees nothing, feels nothing but him, longs for him and him alone, the one and only. Her desires, which have not been corrupted by the empty amusements of an inconstant vanity, set now towards the one end, she wants to be his, in an everlasting bond she wants to come into the happiness she has lacked and enjoy the sum and union of all the pleasures she has longed for. Repeated promises that are for her the seal on the certainty of her hopes, bold caresses that increase her desires, entirely encompass her soul, she drifts in a dumb half-awareness, on the feeling threshold of all delights, she is wrought up to the intensest point. Till at last she stretches out her arms, to embrace all she has wished for—and her beloved leaves her.—Stricken, senseless, she stands before an abyss, all about her is darkness, no prospect, no comfort, no grasp of anything, for *he* has left her in whom alone she felt herself to be alive. She has no eyes for the wide world lying before her, nor for the many who might make good her loss, she feels herself to be alone, abandoned by all the world—and, blindly, marshalled into a narrowness by the fearful plight of her heart, she jumps, to smother her pain in an all-encompassing death.—'See, Albert, that is the story of many a person, and tell me, is that not like a sickness? Nature can find no exit out of the labyrinth of tangled and contradictory forces, and the person must die.

'Woe betide anybody who could look on and say, "The fool! If she had waited, if she had let time do its work, her despair would have settled, some other man would have come along and con-soled her."—It is as if one said, "The fool, dying of a fever! If he'd waited till his strength came back, till his fluids had run clear and the tumult in his blood had quietened, all would have been well and he'd be alive today."'

Albert, who still did not think the analogy very telling, made further objections, among them this: I was only speaking of a sim-ple girl. He could not see how a person of sense, not so limited, with a larger oversight of things, could possibly be excused.—'Friend,' I cried, 'we are all human, and the bit of sense any one of us might have is of little or no use when the passions rage and by the constraints of being human we are put under duress. On the contrary—But more of this some other time,' I said, and seized my hat. Oh, my heart was too full.—And we parted, not having

understood one another. But then here on earth no one easily
understands anyone else.

15 August

It is certain that nothing on earth but love makes a person necessary. I can feel it in Lotte that she would be sorry to lose me, and
it never occurs to the children that I won't be there next day. I
went out today to tune Lotte's piano but couldn't manage to
because the little ones were following me around for a story and
Lotte herself said I should do as they asked. I cut the bread for
their supper, they accept it from me now almost as happily as from
Lotte—and told them the chief part of the tale of the princess who
was waited on by hands.* I learn a good deal doing so, believe me.
I am astonished by the effect it has on them. Because I have to
invent a detail of plot now and then, which I forget the next time,
they tell me at once that the last time it was different, so now I'm
careful to recite the whole thing unchanged in a sing-song voice,
off pat. It has taught me that an author who publishes an altered
version of his story must necessarily harm the work, however
poetically improved it may be. The first impression finds us willing, human beings are made to be persuaded of the most outlandish things—but they hit home in us and stick so fast, woe betide
anyone trying to erase or eradicate them.

18 August

Does it have to be the case that what made a person's felicity will
become the source of his wretchedness?

The full and warm feeling of my heart for living Nature, my
wellspring of abundant joy that turned the world to paradise on
every side, has now become my unbearable tormentor, a spirit of
torture pursuing me wherever I go. Once from the rocks and across
the river and as far as those hills I surveyed the valley in its fruit-
fulness and saw all things about me budding and welling forth;
and I saw those mountains clad from top to toe in dense tall
trees and those valleys shaded in their manifold wanderings by the

loveliest woods and the gentle river gliding through the whispering reeds and on its surface the mirrorings of my beloved clouds
that are wafted across the heavens by the soft evening breeze; and
I heard the birds around me bringing the wood to life and the
gnats danced gleefully in millions in the last red beams of the sun
whose final glances lifted the humming beetle from out of the
grass; and by all the whirring and weaving around me I was alerted
to the ground and to the moss that wrests its nourishment from
the hard rock, and the heath growing down the dry sand slopes
opened to me the holy fires of the inner life of Nature: how I took
all that into my warm heart, felt myself made like a god in the
overflowing fullness, and the figures of the world without end
moved in my soul in splendour, giving life to all things. Colossal
mountains surrounded me, abysses lay before me and streams in
spate hurtled down, the rivers flowed below me and the woods and
the hills resounded and I saw them working and making, one in
another, all the unfathomable forces. And over the earth and under
the heavens there is a seething of the generations of manifold cre-
ation, all, all of it populated with a myriad of shapes. And humans
make themselves safe in little houses and nestle in and have domin-
ion, in their minds, over the wide world! Poor fools, slighting
everything, being themselves so slight.—From the unscaleable
mountains over untrodden wastes to the limits of the unknown
ocean the spirit of the eternal creator blows and delights in every
speck of dust that feels it and lives.—Oh, in those days how often
have I longed with the wings of the crane flying over me for the
shores of the measureless sea, from the foaming beaker of bound-
lessness to drink the rising ecstasy of life and for just one moment
in the cabined energy of my heart to feel one drop of the bliss of
the being that brings forth everything in and through itself.

Brother, even the memory of those hours is a blessing to me.
Even the effort of recalling and saying again those feelings that are
beyond saying lifts my soul above itself and makes me doubly conscious of the anxious state I am in the toils of now.

It is as though a curtain has been drawn back from before my
soul and the scene of unending life transforms itself in front of me
into the abyss of the ever open grave. How can anyone say: this

is—since everything passes, everything rolls by with the speed of lightning, so rarely does a life run the whole course its energies are for but is rapt away with the torrent, sunk and smashed to pieces on the rocks? Every moment eats at you and at those around you whom you love, every moment you are a destroyer and are bound to be. Your most innocent stroll costs a thousand tiny creatures their lives, one footstep shatters the laborious buildings of the ants and stamps a little world into a vile grave. Oh, it is not the great and rare disasters of the world that touch me, not the floods that wash away your villages nor the earthquakes that swallow up your cities. What undermines my heart is the devouring force which lies hidden in the universe of nature and which creates nothing that does not destroy its neighbour and itself. And so I reel in fear, the energies of heaven and earth weaving around me. And all I see is an eternally devouring, eternally regurgitating monster.

21 August

Vainly in the mornings out of heavy dreams coming dimly into consciousness I reach for her; and at nights, deluded by the innocent happy dream that I sat near her on the grass and held her hand and covered it in a thousand kisses, vainly I seek her in my bed. Oh, when still bewildered by sleep I feel with my hands for her and it gives me courage—tears force up in floods from the wellspring of my heart and I weep inconsolably at the prospect of my dire future.

22 August

It is a calamity, Wilhelm, my active powers have waned to a restless lassitude, I can't be idle but nor can I do anything. I have no power of imagination, no feeling for nature, and books sicken me. Being lost to ourselves, we lose everything. I swear to you, at times I wish I were a day-labourer just so that waking in the morning I'd have some prospect in the day ahead, some drive, some hope. Often I envy Albert, I see him up to his ears in papers and imagine I'd be well off being him. Several times I've had the impulse to write to you and the Minister, to petition for that post in the embassy which, you assure me—and I believe you—I would not be refused. For a long time now the Minister has been fond of me and has often urged me to engage myself in one line of work or another; and for perhaps an hour I agree that might be a good idea. But when I think about it and remember the fable of the horse* that tires of his freedom and lets himself be saddled and bridled and gets ridden into the ground—then I don't know what I should do.—And besides, my friend, is not this longing in me for a change in my condition perhaps an inner uneasiness and restlessness that will pursue me wherever I go?

depression ?   28 August

Truly, if my sickness were curable these people would cure it. Today is my birthday* and early in the morning I received a little parcel from Albert. Opening it, the first thing I saw was one of the pale-red ribbons* that Lotte was wearing when I first met her and which I have several times since then begged her to let me have. In the parcel were the two duodecimo volumes of the little Wetstein Homer, an edition I've often wished to own so as not to have to lug the Ernesti* along with me on my walks. See how they anticipate my wishes, they seek out all the little kindnesses of friendship which are a thousand times more valuable than those of the giver who by his dazzling gifts in his vanity only abases us. I have kissed the ribbon a thousand times and deep, deep I breathe in the memory of the ecstasies with which those few happy, gone-for-ever days filled me to overflowing. Wilhelm, the fact is—and I do not complain—life's blossoms are only appearances. So many pass and leave not a trace, so few of their fruits set, so few of those fruits ripen. And yet there are still enough of them—and oh, brother of mine, how can we neglect and disregard ripe fruits and let them rot unenjoyed?

Farewell! It is a splendid summer. Often I sit in the fruit trees in Lotte's orchard and with a long pole detach the pears and reach them down from the very tops. She stands below, I lower them to her and she takes them.

Fool, in your unhappy state are you not deceiving yourself? What will become of you in the rage of this passion without an end? I have no prayer any more but her, no shape or form but hers appears in my imagination, and everything in the world all around me I see only in relation to her. And many a happy hour this gives me— until I have to tear myself away from her again. Oh Wilhelm, what things, and often, my heart drives me to!—When I have sat with her two or three hours and feasted my senses on her shape, her bearing, the heavenly expressiveness of her words, till gradually all my senses are wrought up into a tension, a darkness comes over my eyes, I can scarcely hear, and it takes me by the throat like an assassin and in a wild pounding then my heart strives to give my stifled senses air and only worsens their confusion—Wilhelm, often I don't know whether I'm in the world or not! And—if sorrow does not overwhelm me and if Lotte does not allow me the miserable consolation of weeping out my trouble over her hand— then I have to go, leave, be in the open and wander far this way and that through the fields. What gives me pleasure then is to climb a very steep mountain, force a path through a harsh wood, through hedges that hurt me, through thorns that tear me. Then I feel better—somewhat. And when along the way for thirst and fatigue I can't go on, deep in the night sometimes with the high full moon above me, in a lonely wood, on the bough of a malformed tree, I sit and give my wounded feet relief and slip then at first light into a slumber that further weakens me... Oh Wilhelm, the lonely habitation of a cell, a hair shirt, and a belt of spikes would be comforts then that my soul might languish for. Adieu! I see no end to this misery but the grave.

I must go. I thank you, Wilhelm, for deciding me as I wavered. For two weeks I have been living with the thought of leaving her. I must go away. She is in town again, at a friend's. And Albert— and—I must go away from here.

*10 September**

Such a night that was! Wilhelm, now I can bear anything. I shan't see her again. Oh why can I not fly into your arms and tell you, my dear friend, with tears and raptures what feelings assault my heart! But I sit here and can't get my breath and try to calm myself and await the morning and the horses are ordered for sunrise.

Oh she is peacefully asleep and does not know that she will never see me again. I have torn myself away, in a conversation lasting two hours I was strong enough not to betray my intention. And God, such a conversation!

Albert had promised to be with Lotte in the garden straight after supper. I stood on the terrace under the tall chestnut trees and for the last time watched the sun going down over that sweet valley and the gentle river. I had stood there so often with her watching the glorious spectacle, and now—I walked up and down that beloved avenue of trees. Very often even before I knew Lotte a secret sympathy had held me here and it delighted us at the beginning of our acquaintanceship to discover a shared liking for this spot, which is indeed, in my experience, one of the most romantic that art has ever created.

First between the chestnut trees you have the extensive view— But now I remember, I think I've written you a good deal about it already: how high walls of beech eventually close you in and how, because of an adjoining thicket, the avenue becomes darker and darker until everything ends in an enclosed place and a frisson of solitude. I can still feel how congenial it was to me when I first entered there at high noon. I had very faintly an intimation of the bliss and the pain that setting would witness.

After about half an hour, during which time I had feasted sweetly and consumingly on thoughts of parting and reunion, I heard them approaching up the terrace. I ran down towards them and with a shudder seized and kissed her hand. We had just walked up again when the moon rose from behind the bushy hill. We spoke of this and that and came without noticing near to the sombre bower. Lotte went in and sat down, then Albert by her and

I did likewise, but my unquietness would not let me sit for long. I stood up, paced to and fro in front of them, sat down again. I was in an anxious state. She drew our attention to the lovely effects of the moonlight which, at the far end of the walls of beech, was illuminating the whole terrace: a splendid sight and all the more striking since we were ourselves deeply encompassed in shadows. We were silent, and after a while she began: 'I never go walking in the moonlight, never, without being met by thoughts of my dead, without the feeling of death and of the future coming over me. There is a future life,' she continued, in the tones of a sovereign feeling, 'but, Werther, are we to find one another and know one another again? What is your feeling? What do you say?'

'Lotte,' I said, giving her my hand and my eyes filling with tears, 'we shall see one another again, here and over there we shall!'—I couldn't go on.—Why, Wilhelm, must she ask me that when the fearful farewell was in my heart?

'And whether our departed loved ones know about us,' she continued, 'whether they feel, when things are well with us, that warmly and with love we remember them? Oh my mother's form always hovers around me when in the quiet of the evening I sit there among her children, among my children, and they are gathered around me as they were gathered around her. And when in tearful longing I raise my eyes to heaven and wish that she might look in at us for a moment and see how I have kept my word that I gave her in the hour of her death: to be a mother to her children. And feelingly cry out, "Forgive me, dearest, if I am not to them what you were to them. Oh, I do all I can: they are clothed, fed, and more than that, oh they are loved and cherished. My dear and sainted mother, if you could see the concord we live in you would glorify with fervent thanks the God you prayed to with your last and bitterest tears for the wellbeing of your children."'—

Oh Wilhelm, that is what she said! Who can repeat what she said? How can the cold dead letter represent the heavenly flowering of the spirit? Gently, Albert interrupted her: 'This touches you too deeply, my dear Lotte. I know that your soul is very given to these ideas, but I beg you—' 'Oh Albert,' she said, 'I know you have not forgotten the evenings we sat together at the small round table when Papa was away and we had sent the little ones to bed. Often you had a good book with you and so rarely managed to read anything of it—Was it not a better thing than anything else that her lustrous soul was with us then—the beautiful, gentle, cheerful, always busy woman? God knows how many times I have prostrated myself in tears before Him on my bed and prayed He would make me as she was.'

'Lotte,' I cried, and flung myself down before her, took her hand and wetted it with copious tears, 'the blessing of God and the spirit of your mother are upon you.'—'If you had only known her,' she said, pressing my hand—'she was worthy of being known by you.'—I felt I might cease to be. Never were greater and prouder words spoken over me.—And she continued: 'And this woman had to go from here in the prime of her life when her youngest boy was not six months old. Her illness did not last long, she was peaceful, accepting, only her children grieved her, especially the smallest. When it came near the end, she said, "Bring them up to me," and I led them in, the little ones not understanding, the eldest quite beside themselves, and they stood around the bed and she lifted up her hands and said a prayer over them and kissed them one after the other and sent them away and said to me: "Be their mother!"—I gave her my hand on it—"You are promising a lot, child," she said, "the heart of a mother and the eyes of a mother. I have often seen in your grateful tears that you know what those things are. Have such a heart and such eyes for your brothers and sisters and be faithful and obedient to your father, like a wife. You will be a comfort to him."—She asked where he was, he had gone out to conceal from us his unbearable grief, the man was torn apart by it.

'Albert, you were in the room. She heard someone moving, asked who it was and called you to her, and when she looked—calmly and comforted—at you and me and saw that we should be happy, should be happy together—'Albert clasped her tight, kissed her, and cried, 'We are happy and shall be!'—Albert, the even-tempered man, was entirely discomposed, and I had lost all sense of myself.

'Werther,' she began, 'and this woman had to leave us—God,

when I think sometimes how we let the dearest thing in life be carried off, and no one feels it as keenly as the children who for a long time afterwards lamented that the men in suits of black had carried Mama away.'

She stood up and I awoke and, shaken through and through, remained seated and took her hand.—'We must go,' she said. 'It is time.'—She tried to withdraw her hand, I held it tight.—'We shall see one another again,' I cried, 'and among all the shapes and forms we shall find and know one another again. I am going,' I continued, 'I go willingly and yet, if I had to say it is for ever, I should not be able to bear it. Farewell, Lotte! Farewell, Albert! We shall meet again.'—'Tomorrow, I imagine,' she answered light-heartedly.—How I felt that 'tomorrow'! She did not know, when she withdrew her hand from mine.—They went down the avenue and away, I watched them leaving in the moonlight, threw myself on the earth, and wept all I still could, sprang to my feet, ran out on to the terrace, and there below in the shadow of the tall lime trees I saw her white dress shimmering towards the garden gate, I stretched out my arms and the white dress vanished.

BOOK TWO

WE arrived here yesterday. The Envoy* is out of sorts and for that reason will stay in for a few days. If he weren't so disagreeable, all would be well. Oh, no doubt about it, Fate means to try me hard. Courage! Some lightness of spirit and one may bear anything. Lightness of spirit! I smile at my writing that. Some lightness in the blood perhaps and I'd be the happiest man under the sun. Others with their small strengths and talents strut before me smug and comfortable while I despair of my strengths and my gifts. Dear God, the giver of all this to me, why did you not withhold the half and make me more confident and less demanding instead?

Patience, patience, things will get better. For let me tell you, my dear friend, you were right. Being always with people now, driven hither and thither in the world, seeing what people do and how they behave, I feel much better about myself. The fact is, by our very nature we are bound to compare everything with ourselves and ourselves with everything, and so our happiness or misery lies in the objects we keep company with and nothing in that respect is more dangerous than solitude. Our imagination, naturally impelled to lift itself up and feeding on the fantasies of poetry, conceives of an ascending order of beings, ourselves the lowest, everything outside us appearing more splendid, all others more perfect. And that proceeds quite naturally. We feel very often that we lack this or that and often what we lack some other seems to possess and to him we then also allot all that we have ourselves and a certain imagined easiness as well. And so the happy man, perfectly completed, is a creature of our making.

On the other hand, if we with all our weakness and laboriousness will only keep moving it may very often be the case that we get further with our veering and tacking than others do by plying the oars and sailing with the wind—and—then we really shall feel our worth if we run equal with them or even ahead.

26 November 1771

I am beginning to get by quite tolerably here. The best is I have enough to do, and then the many and various people, all sorts of new characters, make a motley spectacle for my observing soul. I have got to know Count C.,* a man who compels my reverence daily more and more, a large and far-reaching intelligence that, overseeing so much, is not lacking in warmth, and such a radiance of feeling for friendship and love in all his dealings. He took a sympathetic interest in me when I was sent to him on some business and he knew from our first exchanges that we understood one another and that he could speak with me as he couldn't with most. Nor can I sufficiently praise his openness towards me. There's no truer and warmer delight on earth than when a great soul opens itself to you.

24 December 1771

The Envoy causes me much annoyance. I knew he would. He is the most punctilious fool imaginable: step by step, a real old woman, never pleased with himself and for that reason never with anyone else either. I like to dash things off and when it's done I leave it be. But he is quite capable of giving me a paper back and saying, 'This is good but look through it again, you'll surely think of a better word here, a neater expression there.'—Drives me insane. No 'and', no little conjunction, may ever be omitted, and he is mortally averse to inversions, which I do permit myself now and then. Unless you trot out your sentences to the usual tune he can't make head or tail of them. It's a tribulation having anything to do with such a person.

Only my closeness to Count C. makes up for it. Not long ago he told me very candidly how unhappy he is with the slowness and irresoluteness of the Envoy. 'Such people', he said, 'make it hard for themselves and for others; but we have to put up with it, like a traveller who has to get over a mountain. True, if the mountain weren't there, the way would be easier and shorter, but it is there, and we have to get over it.'—

The old man himself senses that the Count prefers me and that annoys him and whenever he has an opportunity he denigrates the Count—whereupon I, naturally, defend him, which makes matters worse. Only yesterday he incensed me—since I was included in the criticism—by saying that the Count would do very well for society matters, he had a light touch and wrote nicely enough, but he was quite lacking in real erudition, like all literary dilettantes. And he gave me a look which said, 'Yourself, for example.' But it did not have the desired effect. I despised the man for thinking and behaving in that fashion and stood up to him and fought back with some vehemence. I said the Count was a man one must respect both for his character and for his knowledge. I said I had never met anyone so successful in broadening his mind and extending it over so many subjects and still with such an engagement in everyday life.—But he had no idea what I meant by that and I took my leave so as not to choke on any more nonsense.

And you are all to blame for talking me into this servitude and preaching me the virtues of being active. Active! I swear, if the man who plants his potatoes and drives into town to sell his corn doesn't do more than me, I'll toil another ten years in the galley I'm chained to now.

And the dazzling wretchedness, the boredom of the hideous folk all rubbing shoulders hereabouts, their obsession with status, how they watch and spy out their chances to get one step ahead— such wretched, lamentable passions, quite without fig-leaf. There's a woman, for example, whose talk with everyone is of her aristocratic family and estate, so that any stranger must think she's a fool dreaming up all sorts of wonders out of a bit of good family and land.—But it's much worse than that: the woman is local and the daughter of a chancery clerk.—I tell you, I do not understand how people can be so witless as to trade themselves so grossly.

But in truth, my dear friend, I see every day more clearly how foolish it is to measure others by oneself. And since I am so occupied with myself and this heart of mine is in such turmoil—oh, I'd gladly let others go their way if they'd only let me go mine.

What irks me most is the stupidity of social relations. Of course, I know as well as anyone how necessary the distinctions between the classes are and what advantages they bring me—but I don't want them in my way when I might have some small enjoyment, some shimmer of happiness, on this earth. Recently on one of my walks I got to know a Fräulein von B.,* a very amiable person who in all the rigidity of life here has managed to preserve a great deal of naturalness. We liked one another as we talked, and when we parted I asked might I call on her at home—which she agreed to so freely I could hardly wait for the appropriate moment to visit. She is not from here and lives with an aunt. I did not like the look of that old lady. I was very attentive to her, directed most of my conversation her way, and in less than half an hour had more or less gathered what Fräulein von B. herself confessed to me later: that her dear aunt in old age lacks everything, has no sufficient fortune, no life of the mind, and no support but the line of her ancestors, no protection but her social status behind which she has barricaded herself, and no enjoyment but looking down from on high over the heads of the bourgeoisie. She is said to have been beautiful in her youth and to have trifled her life away, at first in her conceit tormenting many a poor young man, and in riper years then submitting herself in obedience to an elderly officer who, in return for that and enough to live off, spent the Age of Bronze with her and died. Now in the Age of Iron* she is alone and would have no consideration at all were her niece not so amiable.

good question...

8 January 1772

What manner of people are they whose soul resides wholly in ceremony, whose only thought and striving year after year is how to push in one place higher up the table? And it's not that they have nothing else to do. On the contrary, their tasks accumulate—precisely because by their petty irritations they are kept from advancing the things that matter. Last week on a sleigh-ride there were squabbles and the whole pleasant occasion was ruined. *It's the little thing...*

Fools, that they can't see it is not really a question of what place you occupy and that the man at the top rarely has the major role. Many a king is ruled by his minister and many a minister by his secretary. Who then is the top man? The one, so it seems to me, who oversees all others and is powerful or cunning enough to harness their energies and passions for the execution of his own plans.

20 January

I must write to you, Lotte, here in the parlour of a poor country lodging-house where I have taken shelter from bad weather. In that sad hole D., among people who are strange to me, utter strangers to my heart, trailing around among them, there never came a moment when my heart bade me write to you, and now in this meagre dwelling, in this solitude, in this confinement, snow and hail in a fury at my small window, here you were my first thought. Oh Lotte, as I entered, your living image, the memory of you, so warm and hallowed, came upon me. Dear God, a moment's happiness again!

My dearest friend, if you could see me in all the swirl of distractions! How parched my senses become, not one moment of any abundance of the heart, not one hour that is blessed, nothing, nothing. It's as though I stand before a raree-show and the little men and the little horses shift this way and that before my eyes and I keep asking, is this not an optical illusion? I play my part, or rather I am played, like a marionette, and now and then I seize my neighbour's wooden hand and start back with a shudder. In the evening I resolve to enjoy the sunrise, and I stay in bed; during the day I hope for the pleasures of moonlight, and keep to my room. I don't rightly know why I get up, nor why I lie down.

The yeast is lacking that quickened my life; whatever kept me wakeful deep into the night and woke me from my sleep when morning came, is lost, is gone.*

I've found no female companion here but one, a Fräulein von B.—Dearest Lotte, she is like you, if it is possible to be like you. 'Ah,' you will say, 'the man has taken to flattering,' and that wouldn't be entirely untrue. Of late I have become very charming, since I can't be anything else, very witty, and the ladies say there is no one like me for paying them compliments (and telling them lies, you will add, for without lying it cannot be done, you understand).

But I wanted to tell you about Fräulein B. She has a lot of soul, which looks out at you abundantly from her blue eyes. Her position in society is a burden to her, it satisfies none of the desires of her heart. She yearns to be out of the madding world, and we dream away an hour now and then in country settings of unalloyed bliss. And, oh, we speak of you! How often she has to pay you homage—doesn't have to, does so willingly, delights in hearing about you, loves you.—

Oh, if only I were sitting at your feet in that dear, snug room and our beloved little ones in a scrimmage all around me and if they got too noisy for you I'd gather them close and quieten them down with a fearful fairytale.

The sun is setting in splendour over the snow-brilliant land, the storm has passed, and I—must lock myself back in my cage. Adieu! Is Albert with you? And in what sense? God forgive me the question.

*8 February**

For a week now we have had the most abominable weather, and I am glad of it. In all my time here not one lovely day has dawned without somebody blighting it or ruining it for me. But when it blows and rains good and hard and it's chill and dank, then I say to myself, it can't be worse at home than it is out of doors, or vice versa, and that suits me. If the sun rises in the morning and promises a fine day, I can never refrain from exclaiming, Here's another gift from God they can deprive one another of. There is nothing they won't deprive one another of. Health, a good name, joy, recreation… And mostly out of foolishness, ignorance, and narrow-mindedness, and always—to hear them talk—with the best intentions. I sometimes feel like begging them on bended knee not to tear with such fury at their own hearts.

17 February

I'm afraid my Envoy and I will have to part company before long. The man is absolutely unbearable. His way of working and of conducting business is so ridiculous that I can't refrain from contradicting him and often then I do the thing my way as I think best, which, needless to say, never suits him. On this score he complained to the Court about me and I was rebuked—gently, but nonetheless rebuked—by the Minister and was about to ask to be relieved of my duties when I received a private letter[1] from him, a letter I fell on my knees and worshipped for its nobility, high intelligence, and wisdom. He reproved me for my excessive sensitivity, but rather than wishing to eradicate my extravagant ideas of affecting and influencing others and of driving matters through, he honoured them as youthful courage and confidence and desired only to moderate and direct them where they might come into their own and work as powerfully as they should. I am fortified for a week now and at one with myself. Peace in the soul is a splendid thing, and being happy with oneself. My dear friend, if only that jewel were not as fragile as it is precious and beautiful.

*20 February**

God bless you, my dear ones, and grant to you all the good days He takes from me.

I thank you, Albert, for deceiving me. I was waiting to hear when your wedding-day would be and had resolved on that day with all due ceremony to take down Lotte's silhouette from the wall and bury it under other papers. Now you are joined together and her picture is still there. And there it shall stay. Why not? I know that I am with you both, am there—harmless to you, Albert—in Lotte's heart, hold the second place there which I will and must retain. Oh, I should go raving mad if she were able to forget—Albert, hell opens up in that thought. Albert, farewell. Farewell, angel of heaven. Farewell, Lotte.

---

[1] Our great respect for this excellent gentleman led us to remove the above-mentioned letter, together with another alluded to later, from this collection. Warmest thanks we should have had from our readers, had we included it; but that would not, we thought, have excused the impertinence.

15 March

I have suffered an affront which will drive me away from here. I rage at it. By God, this is beyond repair and the fault is all yours, all of you, for spurring and driving and tormenting me into a situation to which I was unsuited. It serves me right! And serves you right! And so that you won't say yet again that my extravagant ideas ruin everything, I give you here, my dear sir, a plain, straightforward account just as any chronicler of the facts would do.

Count C. loves me, singles me out, that is well known, I have told you a hundred times already. Well, yesterday I dined with him and it happened to be the day on which, towards evening, the noble company of the lords and ladies gathers in his house, which I had not thought of, nor had it occurred to me that we, the inferiors, did not belong there. So I dine with the Count and afterwards we stroll up and down in the great hall, I converse with him and with Colonel B., who has joined us, and the hour of the gathering approaches. God knows, I had not given it a thought. Enter then her more than gracious Ladyship von S. with milord her husband and their flat-chested right-honourable gosling of a daughter, hatched at last and daintily corseted—*en passant* they raise their aristocratic eyes and present their nostrils in the traditional manner, and since I cordially detest the whole breed of them I was ready to say my goodbyes and only waiting till the Count should escape their ghastly twaddle, when my Fräulein B. came in. My heart always lifts up a little when I see her, so I stayed, stood behind her chair, and only after some time did I notice that her conversation with me was less open than usual and somewhat embarrassed. I was struck by that. Is she like the rest of the tribe? I wondered, and felt wounded and would have left, but stayed because I wanted to exonerate her and couldn't believe it and still hoped for a kind word from her—and so on. Meanwhile the company was assembling. Baron F., whose whole wardrobe dates from the coronation of Franz I,* Privy Counsellor R. (here appearing as Herr *von* R.*) with his deaf wife, and the rest, not forgetting the poorly accoutred J. who patches up the holes in his Old Franconian outfit with rags of the latest fashion, they arrive in

droves and I speak to a few of them I am acquainted with, and they
are all very laconic. I thought my own thoughts—and paid attention only to my friend, B. I didn't notice that at the far end of the
hall the women were whispering in one another's ears, that it then
reached the men, that Frau von S. had a word with the Count
(I had all this later from Fräulein B.) till finally he came over and
drew me into the alcove of a window.—'You are aware', he said,
'how bizarre our conventions are. I notice that the company is not
happy to see you here. I wouldn't for anything in the world—'
I interrupted him. 'Your Excellency,' I said, 'a thousand pardons,
I should have thought of it before now and I know you will forgive
me this lapse. I was about to take my leave a while ago, but',
I added with a smile and a bow, 'some evil genius held me back.'—
The Count pressed my hands with a feeling that said everything.
I slipped quietly out of that respectable company, departed, and
drove in a cabriolet to M. and from the hill there watched the sun
go down and read in my Homer the glorious episode in which
Odysseus is given hospitality by the excellent swineherd.* Then
all was well.

Later in the evening I came back to supper. There were still a
few in the parlour, they were in the corner playing dice and had
pushed back the cloth. Then Adelin, a decent man, came in, looked
my way, put down his hat, came over, and said softly, 'You've had
some unpleasantness?'—'Me?' I said.—'The Count ordered you
out.'—'God damn them!' I said. 'I was glad to get some fresh
air.'—'Good that you're not taking it to heart,' he said. 'But it
annoys me, everyone's talking about it.'—Only then did the thing
begin to pain me. Everyone coming in to eat who looked at me,
I thought, that's why they're looking at you. It was like venom
in me.

And then today, wherever I go people commiserate with me,
and when I hear that the envious are now triumphant and are saying, see what happens to those who get above themselves, who are
too clever by half and think themselves free to disregard society's
rules, and more such drivel—it's enough to make you thrust a
knife into your heart. For say what you like about standing on your
own two feet, I'd like to see the man who could bear it when rogues

speak ill of him and are in a position to harm him. When their claptrap is empty, then, of course, you can ignore them.

16 March

I am hounded. Today I met Fräulein B. in the avenue, I couldn't help addressing her and, as soon as we were a little apart from the company, letting her see how her recent behaviour had hurt me.— 'Oh Werther,' she said with some emotion, 'how could you, knowing my heart, think that was what my confusion meant? I suffered for you from the moment I entered the room. I foresaw everything and a hundred times it was on the tip of my tongue to tell you. I knew that Lady S. and Lady T. and their menfolk would sooner leave than remain in the same room as you, I knew that the Count must keep on good terms with them—and the fuss there is now!'— I asked what she meant, concealing my alarm, for at once all that Adelin had told me two days ago ran scalding through my veins.— 'Oh, what it has cost me already!' the sweet girl said, and the tears stood in her eyes.—I could no longer control myself, I was near to falling at her feet.—'Explain!' I cried.—The tears were coursing down her cheeks. I was beside myself. She wiped them away with no effort at concealment.—'You know my aunt,' she began, 'she was there, she watched, and you can imagine how! Werther, yesterday evening and early this morning I suffered a sermon on my relations with you, I had to listen to her disparaging and belittling you and could not—was not free to—do more than half defend you.'

Every word she spoke was a dagger in my heart. She did not sense what a mercy it would have been to keep it all from me. And then she told me how the bad talk would continue and what manner of people would rejoice. How this punishment of my arrogance and of my low opinion of others—which for a long time they had charged me with—would tickle and delight them now. To hear all this from her, Wilhelm, in the voice of truest sympathy—it destroyed me, I am still raging. I wished someone would dare say it to my face so that I might thrust my sword into him, if I saw blood I should feel better. Oh, a hundred times I have seized a knife to let this oppressed heart of mine breathe. I've heard tell of a noble breed of horses that, when they are terribly heated and wrought up, instinctively they bite open a vein, to help themselves breathe. Often I feel like that: I'll open a vein and get myself a freedom that will last for ever. *Wow.*

24 March

I have asked to be relieved of my duties at Court and my request will, I hope, be granted and you will forgive me that I didn't ask your permission first. I had no choice but to leave and I already know what all of you would say to persuade me to stay and so— Sweeten it for my mother, I can't help myself and she will have to accept that I can't help her either. Of course it will grieve her. Her son on his way to becoming Privy Counsellor and Envoy! That fine career no sooner launched than suddenly halted and the little horse back in the stable! Make what you like of it and ponder every combination of circumstances in which I could or ought to have stayed—enough, I'm leaving. And I can tell you where I'm going. Prince —— here, who has a taste for my company, when he heard of my intention he invited me to accompany him to his estate and spend this lovely springtime there. He promises that I shall be left entirely to myself, and since, up to a point, we understand one another, I'll risk it, hoping for the best, and go with him.

Postscript 19 April

Thank you for your two letters. I didn't reply because I was keeping this letter back until my discharge from the Court came through. I was afraid my mother might write to the Minister and make my intention harder to accomplish. But now it is done, I am free to leave—I don't like to tell you how reluctantly they let me go, nor what the Minister wrote: you would all break out in fresh lamentations. The Crown Prince sent me twenty-five ducats for a parting gift together with a note which moved me to tears. So I shan't need the money from my mother that I wrote for recently.

5 May

I leave here tomorrow, and since my birthplace is only about six miles off the route I shall go and see it again and remember the dreamy happiness of the old days. I shall go in at the very gate through which my mother rode out with me when, after the death of my father, she left that beloved homely place and imprisoned herself in her unbearable town. Adieu, Wilhelm, you shall hear of my excursion.

9 May

I made the journey to my native home with all the piety of a pilgrim and many unexpected feelings seized hold of me. I halted my carriage at the great lime tree a quarter of an hour outside the town on the road to S. and told the man to drive on ahead of me. I wanted to be on foot, to enjoy every memory wholly new, livingly, after my own heart. So there I stood under the linden tree which formerly, in my boyhood, had been the goal and the limit of my walks. How different! In those days I yearned in happy ignorance to be out in the unknown world where, as I hoped, there would be much nourishment and enjoyment for my heart and my strivings and longings would be fulfilled and satisfied. Now I come back from the wide world—oh my dear friend, with so many disappointed hopes and so many ruined plans!—I saw the mountains in a line before me which a thousand times had been the object of my desires. I could sit there for hours, heart and soul yearning across to them, to lose myself in the woods and in the valleys offering themselves, like the dawning of a friendship, to my eyes. And when at the prescribed time I had to go back, how reluctantly I left that beloved place!—I approached the town, I greeted all the old and familiar little garden-houses, the new ones I disliked as I did all the other alterations that had been made. I went in at the gate and there at once and entirely I found myself. Dear friend, I shan't go into detail—keenly delightful though everything was to me, it would become monotonous in the telling. I had decided to stay in the market-place, right next to our old house. On the way there

I noticed that the schoolroom, in which an honest old woman had pent up our childhood, was become a shop. I remembered the unease, the tears, the oppression of the feelings, the anxiety around the heart that I suffered in that hole.—Every step I took was remarkable. I doubt any pilgrim in the Holy Land comes upon so many sites of religious remembrance or feels his soul so shaken by holy affections.—One more thing, to stand for a thousand. I followed the river down, as far as a particular farmstead—that was another of my walks, and the places where as boys we used to play ducks and drakes. I had such a lively memory of how I stood there sometimes and gazed after the flowing water, and the wondrous intimations as I followed it, and how adventurous I imagined the country to be into which it was running and how soon I reached the limits of my imagination and yet the water must go further, always further, until I lost myself entirely in the contemplation of an invisible distance.—And see, my dear friend, in the glorious days of our forefathers they were limited and happy in just that fashion. So childlike their feelings and their poetry. When Odysseus speaks of the unmeasured sea and the unending earth, it is so true, human, close, local, and mysterious. How am I helped now by repeating with every schoolboy that the earth is round? A human being needs only a small patch of earth to enjoy himself on—smaller still to lie beneath.

Here I am now at the Prince's hunting lodge. The man is quite liveable with, he has truth and simplicity. He has strange people about him whom I do not understand at all. They don't seem to be rogues but nor do they have the appearance of honest folk. Sometimes they do seem to me honest, and yet I can't trust them.* A pity also that he will often speak of things he has only heard or read about, and then only from the other man's point of view.

And he values my understanding and my talents more than my heart which is, in the end, all I am proud of, the one source of everything, all my strength, all my bliss, all my wretchedness. Oh, anyone may know the things I know—my heart is mine alone.

25 May

I had something in mind which I didn't want to tell you about until it was done, but now that nothing has come of it, I might as well. I wanted to enlist and go to war, it has been my wish for quite some time. That was chiefly why I came here with the Prince, he is a general in service with ——. I told him my plan while we were out walking. He advised against it and the thing would have had to be more of a passion, rather than an idle fancy, to have withstood his arguments.

11 June

Whatever you say, I can't stay any longer. What am I doing here? Time is beginning to drag. The Prince looks after me as well as anyone can and yet I am not in my element. At bottom we have nothing in common. He is a man of understanding—but of a very commonplace understanding. Being with him entertains me no more than if I were reading a nicely written book. I'll stay another week, then I'll begin my wanderings again. The best thing I have done here is my sketching. The Prince has some feeling for art, and would feel more strongly were he not hidebound by the vile nonsense of the academies and all the usual terminology. It maddens me when in the warmth of imagination I bring him to contemplate Nature and Art and he suddenly thinks he knows what's what and blunders in with one old label or another.

16 June*

I am indeed only a wanderer and a pilgrim on the earth. Are you any more than that?

18 June

Where am I going? Let me tell you, in confidence. I have to stay here another fortnight after all and then I have persuaded myself I should like to visit the mines at ——. But really I have no such wish—I want to be nearer Lotte, that is all. And I laugh at my heart—and do its bidding.

29 July

No, it is good, all is well!—Me—her husband! O God, my Maker, had you prepared that bliss for me my whole life would be one continuous prayer. I shan't argue, and forgive me these tears, forgive me my futile wishes.—She, my wife. Had I enfolded her, the dearest creature under the sun, in my arms—A shudder goes through me, Wilhelm, whenever Albert's arm encircles her slim waist.

And dare I say it? Why not, Wilhelm? She would have been happier with me than with him. Oh he is not the man to answer all the desires of her heart. A certain want of feeling, a want of—understand it how you will—that his heart doesn't beat in sympathy at—oh, at that passage in a well-loved book where my heart and Lotte's beat as one. Or the hundred other occasions when we utter our feelings about the doings of some third party. Oh my dear Wilhelm!—True, he loves her heart and soul, and a love like that deserves anything, does it not?—

I have been interrupted by an intolerable person. My tears are dried. I am distracted. Adieu, my dear friend.

4 August

I am not the only one. All human beings are disappointed in their hopes and deceived in their expectations. I visited my good friend, the woman under the linden tree. The eldest boy ran to meet me, his cries of joy brought the mother out. She looked very cast down. Her first words were, 'Oh sir, my Hans has died.'—He was her youngest boy. I was silent.—'And my husband', she said, 'has come back from Switzerland and brought nothing with him and but for people's kindness he would have had to beg his way home, he fell ill of a fever on the way.'—There was nothing I could say to her. I gave the boy something. She begged me to accept a few apples, which I did, and left that place of sad memory.

21 August

From one second to the next my mood changes. Sometimes I have the glimpse and the gleam of a joyous life again—but only for an instant. If I lose myself in dreaming I soon cannot help the thought, What if Albert died? You would... Yes, she would... And I run after this phantom of the mind till it leads me to an abyss I shudder back from.

If I go out at the gate, the way I drove that first time to collect Lotte for the dance, how utterly different that was! Everything, everything has passed. Not one hint of the former world, not one heartbeat of the feelings I had then. I feel as a ghost must feel who returns to the burned-out ruin of a mansion that, as a prince in his prime, he built and furnished with all the gifts of his splendour and dying left in good hope to his beloved son.

3 September

Sometimes it is beyond my comprehension that any other man can love her, is allowed to love her, since I love her solely, with such passion and so completely and know nothing, understand nothing, have nothing but her.

*4 September**

Yes that is how it is. As Nature declines into autumn so it begins to be autumn in me and around me. My leaves are yellowing and the leaves of the neighbouring trees have fallen already. Did I not write to you, soon after I came here, about a farmhand? Again now I enquired after him in Wahlheim and was told he had been dismissed and nobody wanted anything further to do with him. Yesterday I met him by chance on the way to another village, I spoke to him and he told me his story, which moved me, oh how it moved me, and you will easily see why when I tell it you. But what good will it do? Why don't I keep to myself the things that make me fearful and offend me? Why trouble you as well? Why give you

cause of
allow feeling?

these occasions to feel sorry for me and rebuke me? But I shall—and let that also be a part of my fate.

At first the man answered my questions with a quiet sadness which I took to mean he was shy of me; but very soon, as though recognizing both himself and me, he confessed his mistakes and lamented his misfortune more openly. I wish I could bring every one of his words before you, my friend, for you to be their judge. He admitted, indeed he related with a sort of relish and happiness in remembering, that his passion for the woman who employed him had grown daily more strong in him so that in the end he no longer knew what he was doing, nor, as he put it, where to turn with his trouble. He could neither eat, nor drink, nor sleep, he had the sensation of choking, he did things he was not supposed to do and forgot things it was his job to do, he felt pursued by an evil spirit until one day, knowing her to be in an upstairs room, he went up—or rather was drawn up—after her and when she would not listen to his pleading he tried to possess her by force, he did not know what had happened to him, God was his witness, his intentions towards her had always been honourable, he had never wanted anything more fervently than that she should marry him and live her life with him. Having spoken for a while he began to halt like someone who still has things to say but doesn't dare say them. Finally, again with some shyness, he confessed to me what small favours she had granted him and what degree of intimacy she had permitted. Two or three times he broke off and protested in the liveliest fashion that he was not saying it to make her look bad (as he put it), he loved and respected her as before, not a word had he ever said on the subject and he was only telling me now so that I should not think him an utterly wrong and senseless person.—At which point, my friend, I revert to my old theme, as I shall for ever and ever: if only I could present the man to you as he stood—and still stands—before me. If I could only tell you everything right, so that you would feel how I engage myself and am bound to engage myself in his fate. But enough: since you know my fate and also know me, you know only too well why I am drawn to unhappy people and to this unhappy person in particular.

Reading through this letter I see that I forgot to tell you the end

are his
other anecdotes?

of the story—which, however, may easily be imagined. She resisted him, her brother arrived who had long hated him and wanted him out of the house, fearing that if his sister married again his own children would lose the inheritance in which at present, since she is childless, they have good prospects. The brother at once then evicted him and made the matter so public that the woman could not possibly have had him back even had she wanted to. Now she has taken on another farmhand and, so they say, has fallen out with her brother over him too, and it is being said for certain that she will marry him but he—my man—is very determined not to suffer that.

What I am telling you is not exaggerated, nor at all sentimentalized, indeed I may say that I have told it very feebly and have coarsened it by giving it you in our conventional and morally proper language.

This love, fidelity, and passion, therefore, are not a poetic invention. They live, they have their being in greatest purity among the class of people we call uncultured, rude. We, the cultured—cultured for nothing, deformed! Read the story piously, I beg you. I am quiet today, writing it. You can see from my script that I am not scrawling and blotting as I often do. So, you whom I love, read it, and as you read it think this is also the story of your friend. Yes, this is what has happened and will happen to me and I am not half so deserving or so resolute as the poor unfortunate with whom I scarcely dare compare myself.

2.   *Lotte*   5 September*

She had written a note to her husband who was away in the country on business. It began, 'Dearest, my darling, come back as soon as you can, I shall be so happy when you are here again.'—A friend, entering then, brought news that certain circumstances would prevent her husband from returning quite so soon. She left the letter lying and I came across it that evening. I read it and smiled, she asked me why.—'What a gift of the gods imagination is!' I exclaimed. 'For a moment I could pretend it was written to me.'— She turned away, she looked displeased and I was silent.

Sentimentality

It was a long time before I could bring myself to discard the simple blue coat I had on when I first danced with Lotte, but in the end it had become quite unpresentable. And now I have had another one made exactly like the first, the same collar and lapels and new buff-yellow waistcoat and breeches to go with it.

Still the effect is not quite the same. I don't know—perhaps in time I will get to like it better.

12 September*

She was away for a few days, to meet Albert and come back with him. Today I went into her living-room, she came towards me and I kissed her hand with immeasurable gladness

A canary flew from the mirror and alighted on her shoulder.— 'A new friend,' she said, and coaxed him on to her hand. 'I got him for my little ones. He has very sweet ways. Watch. When I give him bread he flutters his wings and picks at it so prettily. And he kisses me too—watch.'

When she offered the little creature her mouth he pressed so winningly between her sweet lips as though well able to feel the bliss he was enjoying.

'Let him kiss you as well,' she said, and handed the bird over.— The little beak made the passage from her mouth to mine and the touch, the pecking, were like a breath, an intimation, of an enjoyment full of love.

'His kiss', I said, 'is not entirely without desire. He seeks nourishment and returns from the empty caress unsatisfied.'

'He eats out of my mouth too,' she said.—She offered him a few crumbs with her lips that smiled in the pleasures of sharing an innocent love with great delight.

I turned my face away. She shouldn't do it—shouldn't excite my imagination with such images of heaven's own innocence and bliss, shouldn't wake my heart out of the sleep into which at times the flatness of life will lull it.—And yet, why not?—She trusts me so, she knows how I love her.

15 September

Oh it drives me mad, Wilhelm, that people can exist and have no sense or feeling for what few things on earth still matter. You remember the walnut trees under which I sat with Lotte and the honest Pastor of St., those glorious walnut trees which, God knows, always filled my soul with the deepest possible satisfaction. How sweet and cool they made the forecourt of the manse, how splendid the branches were, and the memory reaching back to the honest clergymen who planted them so many years ago. One of their names the Schoolmaster often recalled to us, having heard it from his grandfather, and such a good man he is said to have been and his memory was always sacred to me under those trees. I tell you, the Schoolmaster had tears in his eyes when I heard from him yesterday that they have been chopped down.—Chopped down! I shall go mad with rage. I could murder the wretch who first raised the axe against them. I who could grieve to death if two such trees grew by my house and one of them died of age—I have to witness this! But one thing, dearest friend—some human feeling: the whole village is angry, and I hope the Pastor's wife* will feel in the scanting of butter, eggs, and other signs of goodwill just what a wound she has dealt her parish. For it is her, the wife of the new Pastor (our old one died), a scrawny, sour creature who has every reason to feel no sympathy with the world since no one has any sympathy for her. She's a fool with pretensions to learning who meddles in Bible studies, works hard in the fashionable moral-critical way* for the reformation of Christianity, and shrugs her shoulders at Lavater's enthusiasm. Her health is ruined and for that reason she has no delight in anything on God's earth. Only such a creature could possibly chop down my walnut trees. Do you see, I am beside myself. Imagine, the falling leaves make her forecourt dirty and damp, the trees block her light, when the nuts are ripe the boys throw stones up at them and that gets on her nerves, it disturbs her in her cogitations on the relative merits of Kennicott, Semler, and Michaelis.* When I saw the people in the village so unhappy, especially the older ones, I said, 'Why did you let her?'—'Round here,' they said, 'if the Elder wants a thing, what can we do?'—It didn't go right for him, however. The Village Elder and the Pastor—who himself wanted something from his wife's crackpot ideas, which it must be said will never make him rich—thought they would share the timber at least, but the Chancellory got wind of it and said, 'Ours, not yours'—for they had an ancient claim on the part of the manse grounds where the trees stood and sold the timber to the highest bidder. So Pastor and Elder lost out. Oh, if I were Prince, I'd soon see to it that the Pastor's wife, the Village Elder, and the Chancellory—Prince!—If I were Prince what would I care about the trees in my land?

10 October

I look into her black eyes and all is well. And do you see that what upsets me is that Albert seems not to be made as happy as he—hoped—as I—surely would expect to be—if—I don't like using dashes but here I can't express myself any other way—and, it seems to me, this way is clear enough.

> dashes
Todd

12 October

Ossian has displaced Homer in my heart.* What a world the splendid singer leads me into! I wander the moors in the howling of the storm-wind that marshals ancestral ghosts in a wreathing mist in the unsteady light of the moon. From off the mountain in the bellowing of the torrent through the trees, in the dispersing wind, I hear the groans of the spirits in their caves and the keening of the girl as around the four grass-overgrown, moss-covered stones that house her beloved, fallen nobly, she grieves herself to death. And I find him there, the grey, wandering bard who seeks the footsteps of his fathers on the wide moor and finds, oh! their sepulchral stones and turns his face in sorrow to the evening star as it sinks into the rollers of the sea and in his hero soul past ages come alive again when a kindly light shone upon the dangers facing the brave and the moon lit up their ship returning garlanded with victory. I read the deep grief on his brow, I see him, the last and forsaken relict of a glorious people, tottering exhausted towards the grave and in the impotent presence of his shadowy dead still battening for sustenance on joys that burn and hurt. He bows his face over the cold earth, over the tall, wind-ridden grass, and cries: 'The traveller will come,* will come, who knew me in my beauty and will ask, "Where is the singer, Fingal's noble son?" He treads over my grave and asks for me on earth in vain.'—Oh, friend, like a faithful squire I'd like to draw my sword and speedily free my prince from the torment of the slow agony of his life and then dispatch my own soul after him, the liberated hero.

19 October

Oh the gap, the fearful gap, I feel here in my breast!—Often I think if once, just once, I could press her to my heart the gap would all be filled.

26 October

Wilhelm, I feel certain—more and more certain—that the life of a living creature matters little, matters very little. A friend of Lotte's arrived and I went into the next room, took up a book and couldn't read it, then my pen, to write. I could hear them talking softly. They were recounting things of no very great importance: town news, a woman getting married, another ill, very ill—'She has a dry cough, the bones are showing through her face, she keeps fainting, I wouldn't bet a penny on her life,' said the friend.—'So-and-so is very poorly too,' said Lotte.—'Yes,' said the friend, 'he has swollen up.'—And my lively imagination transported me to the bedside of these poor people—I saw how reluctant they were to turn their backs on life, how they—Wilhelm, and those two women were speaking of them just as anyone would who tells you—that a stranger is dying.—And when I look around and see the room and all about me Lotte's clothes and Albert's papers and the furniture and even this inkwell, things I am so attached to, and I think: See what you are now to this house. All in all. Your friends respect you. Often you are a joy to them and your heart feels it could not be without them and yet—if now you went away, if you left this circle, how long, for how long would they feel the gap that the loss of you had torn in their lives?—Oh, a man is such a passing thing that even in the place where he has the real certainty of his existence, where he makes the only true impression of his presence, in the remembrance, in the souls of his loved ones, even there he will be extinguished, even from there he will disappear— and before very long.

27 October

How can we matter so little to one another? It makes me want to tear open my breast and break through the skull into the brain. Oh the love, joy, warmth, and delight that I cannot bring nobody else can give me, nor with a whole heart full of bliss can I make anyone happy who stands before me cold and impotent.

*27 October, evening**

I have so much and my feeling for her devours everything, I have so much and without her everything is nothing.

30 October

Have I not a hundred times been on the point of taking her in my arms! God only knows what it does to a man to watch such lovableness passing before him and not be allowed to reach out for it. Is not reaching out the most natural of human impulses? Don't children reach out for everything they notice?—Why shouldn't I?

3 November

God knows, very often I lie down with the wish, indeed sometimes with the hope, never to wake: and in the morning I open my eyes, see the sun again, and am wretched. Oh, if it were only a moodiness and I could blame the weather, some third person, some failed enterprise, the unbearable weight of discontent would rest only half on me. But alas, I feel all too certainly that the fault is mine alone—Not fault! But simply that deep in me the source of all misery resides as did formerly the source of all bliss. Am I not still the man who once soared on the wings of abundant feeling, whose every step opened up a paradise, who had a heart to embrace the whole world in love? That heart is dead now, raptures no longer flow from it, my eyes are dry and my senses, no longer bathed by refreshing tears, contract my brow in anxiety. I suffer greatly, for I have lost what was the whole joy of my life—the holy, enlivening power* by which I brought worlds into being all around me. That power has gone.—When I look through my window at the distant hill as the morning sun comes over it, breaks through the mist, and illuminates the quiet meadows of the valley floor and the soft river serpents towards me through its leafless willows—oh, when Nature in her glory stands before me rigid as a lacquered little picture and all the delight of it cannot pump one drop of bliss from my heart up to my brain and my poor self, all that it is, stands before the countenance of God like a dried-up well and a broken pitcher.* Often I have thrown myself on the earth and prayed God for tears as a countryman prays for rain when the sky above him is brass* and the ground around him parching.

But alas, I feel it—God does not give rain and sunshine at our importuning, and those times that I remember in torment now, why were they so blessed but because I waited in patience for His spirit and the joy He poured over me I received it with a whole and fervently thankful heart!

8 November

She has reproached me for my excesses—oh, in such a lovable fashion! Excesses! That occasionally I may let a glass of wine become a bottle.—'Don't do it,' she says. 'Think of Lotte.'—'Think of you!' I said. 'Do you need to tell me to do that? Think! I don't *think* of you. You are always present in my soul. Today I was sitting where you stepped from the carriage recently—' She talked of something else so that I wouldn't develop my theme. Friend, I am lost. She can do what she likes with me.

15 November

I thank you, Wilhelm, for your kind sympathy, for your well-meant advice, and I beg you not to say any more. Let me bear it to the end, in all this travail I do still have the strength to see it through. I honour religion, as you know, I sense that for many who are weary it is a staff and for many who thirst it is refreshment. But—can it, must it, be that for everyone? When you consider the great world you see thousands for whom it never was, thousands for whom it never will be, whether they were preached it or not, so why should it be those things for me? Does not the Son of God Himself say* that they will be with Him whom the Father has given to Him? And if I am not given to Him? If the Father wants to keep me for Himself, as my heart tells me He does?—I beg you not to misconstrue this, do not see any sort of mockery in these innocent words, I am laying out my whole soul before you, or I should have said nothing since I'm never eager to speak on subjects everyone knows as little about as I do. What else is it but the fate attendant on being human—to suffer one's measure, to drain the cup?—And if the chalice was too bitter* for the human lips of the God of heaven why should I play a bragging part and pretend I find it sweet? And why should I be ashamed in the frightful moment when my whole existence trembles between to be and not to be, when the past flashes like lightning over the black abyss of the future and everything around me founders and the world goes down with me—Is it not the voice of a creature driven wholly into itself, losing itself, toppling unstoppably down, in the inner depths of its energies vainly labouring to rise—the voice that asks through grating teeth, 'My God, my God why hast thou forsaken me?'* And am I to be ashamed of that moment, am I to be afraid of it, when He could not escape it Who rolls up the heavens like a cloth?*

21 November

She does not see, she does not feel that she is preparing a poison that will be the undoing of me and of her—and with a carnal delight I gulp the cup she hands me for my destruction. What do the kind looks mean that she often—often?—no, not often but sometimes bestows on me, the favour with which she receives some involuntary expression of my feeling, the pity for my suffering that marks her brow?

Yesterday as I was leaving she gave me her hand and said, 'Adieu, dear Werther.'—Dear Werther! It was the first time she had ever called me dear and it pierced me through and through. I repeated it to myself a hundred times and last night, getting ready for bed and muttering all sorts of things, I suddenly said, 'Goodnight *dear* Werther'—and laughed out loud to hear it.

*22 November**

I cannot pray: 'Let me have her.' Yet often she seems to be mine. I cannot pray: 'Give her to me.' For she is someone else's. I explicate my pain this way and that—if I let myself go, there'd be a whole litany of theses and antitheses.

24 November

She feels what I am suffering. Today her look went deeply through my heart. I found her alone, I said nothing and she looked at me. And I no longer saw loveliness in her, no longer the shining forth of her spirit, all that vanished before my eyes. The look I felt entering me was of a different order, expressive through and through of the most heartfelt understanding and sweetest sympathy. Why was it forbidden me to throw myself at her feet or take her in my arms and answer her with a thousand kisses? She turned for a refuge to her piano and accompanied her playing with a sweet murmuring, almost under her breath, of melodious sounds. Never have I seen her lips so desirable, they seemed to open in thirst to drink the sweet notes welling up from the instrument while from her pure mouth it was their secret echo that issued forth—Oh, if only I could tell you how it was!—I gave in, I bowed my head and swore: Never will I dare to press a kiss on those lips where the ghosts of heaven play—And yet—I want—There, do you see? It stands like a dividing wall before my soul—that bliss—and then extinction, to atone for the sin—Sin?

*26 November**

Sometimes I say to myself: Your fate is unique, think the others fortunate—none has been tormented as you have. Then I read some poet of the ancient times and it is as though I were looking into my own heart. I have to bear so much. Oh, have there been people before me who were so wretched?

30 November

It seems decided that I shall never recover myself! Everywhere I go I have encounters that utterly discompose me. Today—oh destiny, oh humankind!

I was walking along the river at midday, I had no appetite for food. Everything was desolate, a damp, cold west wind blew from the mountains and grey rainclouds advanced into the valley. At a distance I saw a man in a shabby green coat scrabbling around among the rocks as though looking for herbs. Getting nearer, when he heard me and turned round, I saw a most interesting face whose chief characteristic was a still sorrow and which, apart from that, looked simply good-natured. His black hair was pinned up in two rolls, with a substantial plait of it hanging down his back. Since his dress seemed to denote a person of the lower classes I thought he would not take it amiss if I noticed his occupation, and accordingly I asked him what he was looking for.—He answered, with a deep sigh, 'I am looking for flowers—and can't find any.'—'But it's not the season,' I said with a smile.—'There are so many flowers,' he said, coming down to me. 'In my garden there are roses and two kinds of honeysuckle, one of them my father gave me, they grow like weeds, I've been two days looking for them and cannot find them. There are always flowers at home, yellow and blue and red, and the centaury blooms very prettily. Not one of them can I find.'—I detected something not right, and so in a roundabout way I asked him what he wanted the flowers for.—His face twitched in a strange smile.—'Don't tell on me,' he said, and put a finger to his lips. 'I have promised my sweetheart a bouquet.'—'That is good,' I said.—'Oh,' he said, 'she has many other things besides. She is rich.'—'But she likes your bouquet,' I replied.—'Oh,' he continued, 'she has jewels and a crown.'—'And what is she called?'—'If the States General* would pay me,' he answered, 'I'd be a different person. Yes, there was a time when all was well with me. Now I'm finished. Now I'm—' He looked heavenwards with tears in his eyes and that said everything.—'So you were happy once?' I asked.—'Oh I wish I were again. All was well with me then, all so jolly, I was happy as the day is long.'—'Heinrich!' cried an old woman coming down the path. 'Heinrich, where have you been? We looked everywhere for you. Come and eat.'—'Is this your son?' I asked, stepping towards her.—'So he is,' she answered. 'My poor son. God has laid a heavy cross upon me.'—'How long has he been like this?' I asked.—'So quiet,' she said, 'only the last six months. Thank God that he has got to be only as bad as this. For a year before, he was raving, he lay in chains in the madhouse. Now he wouldn't hurt a soul. It's only that he's bothered all the time with emperors and kings. He was such a good and quiet man, he helped look after me, wrote a very nice hand, and suddenly he took to pondering, fell into a hot fever, then into a raving, until he became as you see him now. Oh sir, if I were to tell you—' I interrupted her stream of words with the question, 'When was this famous time of his happiness and wellbeing?'—'The silly man,' she exclaimed with a smile full of pity, 'he means the time when he was out of his mind, he never stops glorifying it—it's the time when he was in the madhouse and knew nothing of his state.'—That struck me like a thunderbolt. I pressed some money into her hand and left her hurriedly.

When you were happy, I exclaimed, walking quickly towards the town, when you were happy as the day is long!—God in heaven, have you fated men to be happy only before they have any understanding and only after they lose it again?—Poor wretch, but then also how I envy you the confusion and clouding of the mind in which you languish. You go forth in hope to pick flowers for your queen—in winter—and grieve that you find none and do not understand why you can't find any. And I—I go forth without hope, without purpose, and return as I went out.—You think you know what manner of man you would be if the States General paid you. It is a blessed creature who can blame some earthly obstacle for his want of happiness. You never feel that in the ruins of your heart and the debris of your brain lies the misery not all the kings on earth could cure you of!

   Die without hope of comfort whoever mocks the sick man journeying to the farthest wells for a draught that will only worsen his sickness and end his life in even greater pain! Or whoever disdains the man who in the oppression of his heart, to be rid of the pangs of conscience and to cast off the sorrows that lie upon his soul, makes a pilgrimage to the Holy Sepulchre. Every piercing footstep on harsh paths is a drop of assuagement for his anxious soul and after every day's hard march the burden of tribulations on his heart, when he lies down, is lighter.—And by what right do you—the cushioned and the wordy—call him deluded?—Deluded!—O God, you see my tears! You made man poor enough, why then give him brothers who rob him of the bit he has, his bit of faith in you, in you and your all-encompassing love? For the faith in a healing root, in the tears of the vine, what else is that but faith in you who set in everything around us the powers of healing and relief we are so frequently in need of? Father, whom I do not know, who once filled all my soul and have now turned away your countenance from me, call me to you, be silent no longer, your silence will not deter this thirsting soul.—And would any human being, any father, be able to be angry if his unexpectedly returning son* fell upon his neck and cried, 'I am home, Father, do not be angry that I have broken off the journey which it was your will I should endure longer. The world is everywhere the same—on toil and trouble come reward and joy—but what is that to me? I am well only where you are and only in your sight do I wish to suffer and enjoy.'—And you, dear Heavenly Father, would you turn him away?

1 December

Wilhelm, the man I wrote to you about, that happy unhappy man, was a clerk with Lotte's father and a passion for her which he nourished, hid, confessed, and for which he was dismissed, sent him raving mad. Feel now in these dry words how the story overthrew my mind when Albert recounted it to me as calmly as you perhaps read it.

4 December

I beg you—See, I am finished, I cannot bear it any longer. Today I was sitting with her—sitting, and she was playing the piano, many and various melodies, and all the expressiveness, all—all!—What can I say?—Her little sister was dressing her doll on my knee. Tears came to my eyes. I bowed my head and caught sight of her wedding ring—my tears flowed—And suddenly she launched into the old celestially sweet tune, quite suddenly, and through my soul went a feeling of comfort and memories of the past, of the times when I heard that tune, the dark times in between, in which I suffered humiliation and my hopes foundered, and then—I paced up and down in the room, my heart was choking under the assault of feelings.—'For God's sake,' I said, with great vehemence bearing towards her, 'for God's sake, stop!'—She stopped, and stared at me.—'Werther,' she said, with a smile that transfixed my soul, 'Werther, you are very sick, you have no appetite for your favourite dishes. Go now. I beg you, calm yourself.'—I tore myself away from her and—God, you see my wretchedness and will end it.

6 December

How the apparition pursues me. Waking and dreaming it occupies all my soul. Here when I close my eyes, here in my head where the inner vision forms, are her black eyes. Here, I cannot express it to you. I close my eyes and hers are there—like a sea, like an abyss, they lie before me, in me, they wholly occupy the senses in my head.

What is this thing, the vaunted demigod, a man? Does he not lack powers precisely when he needs them most? And when he soars in joy and sinks down in sorrow is he not stopped in both and fetched back into dumb, cold consciousness precisely when he had longed to lose himself in the fullness of infinity?

THE EDITOR TO THE READER

I very much wish that our friend had left us enough documents of his remarkable last days for me not to be obliged to interrupt the succession of his surviving letters by acting as narrator.

I have made it my business to gather exact information from the mouths of those who could have a good knowledge of his story—which is straightforward, and except in a few trivial details all versions of it tally. Opinions differ and judgements are divided only when it comes to the ways of thinking and feeling of the people involved.

All we can do is conscientiously recount what by dint of repeated efforts we have been able to find out, inserting the letters left by our departing friend and giving proper importance to every least note that has come to light; especially since it is so difficult to uncover the very particular true motivations of even one action when it occurs among people who are not of the common run.

Grievance and unhappiness rooted deeper and deeper in Werther's soul, intertwined there ever more tightly, and at length took possession of his whole being. The harmony of his mind was quite destroyed, an inward heat and vehemence, which wrought up and disarrayed all his natural energies, caused the most unpleasant reactions in him, exhausting him, and by his efforts to rise up again his courage was sapped even more than by the troubles he had fought against so far. The anxieties besetting his heart consumed the last energies of his mind, his liveliness, his keen intelligence; he became sad company, ever more unhappy and ever more unjust the unhappier he became. So say Albert's friends, at least. They insist that Werther who, so to speak, daily consumed all he owned and every evening suffered and wanted, could not be the judge of a calm and pure man who, having come into the possession of a long-wished-for happiness, was acting now to secure it for the future also. Albert, they say, had not changed in so short a time, he was the same man Werther had known from the beginning and had so esteemed and honoured. He loved Lotte above all else, he was proud of her and wished that everyone should acknowledge her to be a most wonderful person. How then could he be blamed for wanting to safeguard her from even the appearance of any suspicion and for having at that moment no desire to share this most precious possession even in the most innocent fashion with anyone else? They concede that Albert would often leave his wife's room when Werther was with her, but not out of hatred or dislike of his friend, only because he felt that his presence oppressed him.

Lotte's father had fallen ill and was confined to the house, he sent his carriage and she drove out to him. It was a fine winter's day, the first snow had fallen, the country lay deep in it.

Werther followed Lotte the next morning, to accompany her home if Albert didn't come for her.

The clear winter weather had little effect on his troubled spirits, a dumb oppression lay upon his soul, sad images had established themselves in him and there was no movement in his mind except from one painful thought to the next.

Living himself in an eternal discontent, the state other people were in also seemed to him more worrying and confused. He believed he had troubled the lovely relationship between Albert and his wife, he reproached himself for this but mixed in with the self-reproaches was a secret grudge against the husband.

Even as he walked, his thoughts turned to this subject. 'Oh yes,' he said to himself, grinding his teeth—'Close, friendly, tender, and sympathetic in all his dealings with her, a lasting peaceful fidelity! Complacent satisfaction, that's what it is, and indifference. Does not any wretched piece of business engage him more than the woman who is so precious? Does he know how fortunate he is? Can he value her as she deserves? He has her—well then, he has her—I know that, just as I know other things, I believe I have got used to the thought, it will still drive me mad, it will still be the death of me—And has his friendship to me held good? Does he not think my devotion to Lotte a trespass on his rights and my attentiveness to her a silent reproach? I know it full well, I feel it, he does not like to see me, he wishes me removed, my presence is irksome to him.'

Often he halted his rapid walking, often he stood still and seemed about to turn back, but went on his way, on and on, and amid these thoughts and soliloquies he arrived at last, as it were against his will, at the hunting lodge.

He went in, asked after the old man and Lotte, found the household in some commotion. The oldest boy told him that something bad had happened over in Wahlheim—a farmhand had been murdered!—This did not make any impression on him.—He went into the living-room and found Lotte trying to dissuade her father who despite his illness wished to go over and investigate the deed at the scene itself. It was not yet known who had done it, they had discovered the victim that morning outside the door, they had their suspicions: the dead man was the farmhand of a widow, she had previously employed someone else who had left the house discontented.

When Werther heard this, he started up violently.—'Can it be true?' he cried. 'I must go over there, and at once.'—He hurried towards Wahlheim, all his memories revived and he did not for one moment doubt that the perpetrator was the man he had so often spoken to and grown so fond of.

Having to pass through the lime trees to reach the public house where they had laid the body, he filled with horror at the once so beloved place. That threshold on which the local children had so often played was fouled with blood. Love and fidelity, the finest human feelings, had transformed themselves into violence and murder. The strong trees stood leafless in a hoarfrost, the lovely hedges that bowed over the low wall of the churchyard were bare, and the gravestones, covered with snow, showed through the gaps.

As he approached the house, outside which the whole village had gathered, there was a sudden shouting. At a distance a troop of armed men could be seen and everyone cried that they were bringing in the murderer. Werther looked and soon had no doubts. It was indeed the farmhand who had so loved the widow and whom some time ago he had met wandering in a speechless anger and an untold despair.

'Unhappy man,' Werther cried, approaching the prisoner, 'oh, what have you done?'—The man looked at him and for a while said nothing. Then in a level voice he answered: 'No one will have her and she will have no one.'—They took him under guard into the public house and Werther hurried away.

By this violent and terrible encounter everything in his being was thrown into turmoil. Instantly he was torn out of his sadness, his resentment, his fatalistic indifference. An overwhelming sympathy possessed him and he was seized by an unspeakable desire to save the man. He felt him to be so unhappy, found him, even as malefactor, so guiltless, sank himself so deeply into his situation that he surely believed he could persuade others too. He wished to speak up for him, already the liveliest possible address was on his lips, he hurried towards the hunting lodge, under his breath as he went already helplessly muttering all the things he would put to the Land Steward.

Entering the living-room he found Albert present, which disconcerted him for a moment; but then he recovered and ardently presented his views to the Steward. With the greatest liveliness, passion, and truth he advanced everything that one human being may say to excuse another, but the Steward, occasionally shaking his head, remained, as would be expected, unmoved. Indeed, he did not let our friend finish, spoke energetically against him, and said he was wrong to come to the defence of a cold-blooded murderer. In that way, he argued, all laws would be annulled, the security of the state would be demolished, and besides, he added, in such a case he could do nothing without taking upon himself the very gravest responsibility, everything must proceed in proper order and in the prescribed fashion.

Werther still did not give up, but begged the Land Steward at least to turn a blind eye if the man were helped to escape. Again the Steward said no. Albert, finally joining in the conversation, sided with the old man. Werther was overridden and in terrible torment he left, the Steward having more than once said to him, 'No, he cannot be saved.'

These words must have struck home very forcibly, as may be seen from a note found among his papers and certainly written on that day: 'Unhappy man, you cannot be saved. I see for sure that we cannot be saved.'

The things Albert had said last in the presence of the Land Steward concerning the prisoner were deeply antipathetic to Werther. He thought he detected some hostility towards himself in them; and although, thinking more about it, his own intelligence told him that both men might be right, he still felt he must surrender his innermost being if he admitted and conceded it.

A note referring to this and perhaps expressing his entire relationship with Albert was found among his papers: 'Again and again I say to myself, he is a good and dependable man, it tears my heart and soul out nevertheless and I can't be fair.'

Since it was a mild evening, the weather inclining towards a thaw, Lotte and Albert went back together on foot. As she walked, she glanced around her, as though she were missing Werther's company. Albert began to talk about him and, with all fairness, he censured him. He touched on his unhappy passion and wished it might be possible to put him more at a distance.—'I wish it for our sakes too,' he said, 'and', he continued, 'I beg you to give some other direction to his conduct towards you, reduce the frequency of his visits. People have noticed and I know that in some quarters there has been talk about it.'—Lotte said nothing and Albert seemed to have taken her silence to heart. At least, from then on he did not mention Werther to her and if she mentioned him he broke off the conversation or moved it elsewhere.

The vain attempt to save the unfortunate farmhand was the last flaring-up in Werther of a flame and a light that were being extinguished. He sank all the deeper into pain and inactivity; and he was almost beside himself when he heard that he might even be summoned as a witness against the man, who had turned to denying his deed.

Every unpleasant thing that had ever happened to him in his public life, the humiliation at the embassy, every other thing he had ever failed at, that had ever insulted him, turned and turned again in his soul. All this worked in him as a justification for doing nothing, he felt cut off from any prospect, incapable of marshalling any of the resources with which one might arm oneself to deal with the business of ordinary life; until at last, utterly given up to his strange feelings and ways of thinking and to his unending passion, in the eternal sameness of his sad dealings with the lovable and beloved woman whose peace of mind he was disturbing, in an assault on his own energies, wearing them out without purpose or prospect, he shifted nearer and nearer to a sad end.

A few of the letters he left, which we interpolate here, are a most powerful testimony of his confusion, passion, restless drive, and striving, and of his weariness unto death.

12 December

Dear Wilhelm, I am in a state such as those unfortunates must have been in who were believed to be driven hither and thither by an evil spirit. Sometimes it seizes me, it is not fear or desire—it is an inner nameless raging that threatens to tear open my breast and that throttles me. Alas, alas, and then I drift about among the terrible night-scenes of this season that is hostile to humans.

Yesterday evening it forced me out. There was a sudden thaw, I heard the river had burst its banks, all the streams were swollen and down from Wahlheim my lovely valley flooded. That night after eleven I ran out. A terrible spectacle—from the rock I could see the waters milling and swirling in the moonlight over the ploughlands, the meadows, and the hedges and the whole wide valley upstream and down become one storming sea under a howling wind. And when the moon stepped forth again and lay above the black cloud and the waters rolled and resounded before me in her terrible and splendid light: the terror came over me and again a yearning. Oh, I stood over the abyss with open arms and breathed down, down, and lost myself in the ecstasy of committing my torments and my sorrows down there in a tempest and to vanish in a roaring like the waves! Oh!—and I could not do it, could not lift my foot from the ground and make an end of all those torments!—My time has not yet run out, I feel it. Oh Wilhelm, how gladly I'd have given up my being human and shredded the clouds with the storm-wind and seized hold of the flooding waters! Oh, shall I not one day in my prison be accorded that ecstasy?—

And looking down mournfully on a spot where I once rested under a willow with Lotte, walking on a hot day—that too was flooded and I scarcely even recognized the willow. Oh Wilhelm— and I thought, her meadows and around the hunting lodge and around our bower, I thought how discomposed it will all be now by the river in its spate. And a ray of the sunlight of the past shone in as to a prisoner a dream of flocks, pastures, public honours! I stood still.—I don't blame myself, for I do have the courage to die.—I could have—Now I sit here like an old woman who gleans her firewood from the hedges and her bread at people's doors to extend and lighten her joyless and languishing existence a short while longer.

14 December

My dear friend, what is this? My own self frightens me. Is not my love for her the holiest, purest, and most brotherly love? Have I ever once felt a forbidden desire in my soul?—I shan't claim— And now, dreams! Oh how true was the human feeling that under-stood such contradictions to be the work of alien forces! Last night, I tremble to say it, I held her in my arms, I pressed her hard against my heart and with unending kisses closed upon her mouth that was whispering her love. She had a wildness in her eyes and into it I plunged. God, is it punishable that I still feel the bliss and call back upon myself with full intensity the fires of that joy? Lotte! Lotte!—And I am done for. My senses are in confusion, for a week I have been unable to think straight, my eyes are full of tears. I feel well nowhere and as well off here as there. I desire nothing, I demand nothing. I'd be better if I left.

At this time and in such circumstances the decision to leave the world had grown ever stronger in Werther's soul. Since his return to Lotte it had always been his last prospect and hope; but he had told himself it must not be a precipitate and hasty act, he would take the step in all conviction and with the calmest possible resolve.

His doubts, his quarrel with himself, are apparent in a note which is very likely the beginning of a letter to Wilhelm and which, undated, was found among his papers.

'Her presence, her own fate, the sympathetic interest she takes in mine, force the last tears from my cauterized brain.

'To lift the curtain and step behind it—that is all! And why the hesitating and the apprehension? Because we do not know how things look behind that curtain? Because there is no return?* And because it is in the nature of our minds to suspect confusion and darkness wherever we can't know anything definite.'

In the end he became more and more familiar with his unhappy idea, he made friends with it, his intention grew firm and irrevocable—as witness the following ambiguous letter to his friend.

20 December

I thank you in your love for me, Wilhelm, that you took up my words that way. Yes, you are right: I'd be better if I left. Your suggestion I should return to you doesn't suit me quite; at least, I'd like to make a detour first, especially since there's hope the frost will last and that the going will be good. Also I'm very touched that you would come and fetch me—only wait another couple of weeks until you hear from me again with more details. It is necessary that nothing shall be plucked until it is ripe. And one way or another fourteen days make a difference. Tell my mother to pray for her son and that I ask her forgiveness for all the trouble I have caused her. In the end it was my fate to bring sorrow to those I should have gladdened. Farewell, my dear, dear friend. All the blessings of heaven be upon you. Farewell.

The events in Lotte's soul at this time, her feelings towards her husband and her unhappy friend, are things we scarcely dare put into words; though knowing her character we can in silence form some idea of them and any womanly beautiful soul may think itself into hers and feel with her.

This much is certain, in herself she was firmly resolved to put Werther at a distance, and if she delayed it was out of her friendship's heartfelt desire to spare him, because she knew what it would cost him, indeed, that he would find it almost impossible. But at this time she came under greater pressure to act in earnest; her husband never spoke about the relationship, just as she herself never had, which obliged her all the more to prove to him by the deed that her feelings were worthy of his.

On the same day that Werther wrote the letter to his friend included above—it was the Sunday before Christmas—he called on Lotte in the evening and found her alone. She was busy collecting together a few playthings that she had prepared as Christmas presents for her youngest brothers and sisters. He spoke of the pleasure the children would feel and remembered how in times long past he had himself been transported to paradise by the surprise opening of a door and the appearance of the decorated tree with its candles, sweets, and apples.—'There's a present for you too,' said Lotte, hiding her embarrassment under a sweet smile, 'if you are very good—a wax taper, and something else.'—'And what do you mean by very good?' he cried. 'What am I supposed to be like? Dearest Lotte, what *can* I be like?'—'Thursday evening', she said, 'is Christmas Eve, the children are coming and my father as well, everyone will have their presents. You come too, but not before.'—Werther started.—'I beg you,' she continued, 'we have reached this point, for my own peace of mind, I beg you, things cannot, cannot remain as they are.'—He averted his eyes, walked up and down in the room, muttering through his teeth her 'things cannot remain as they are'. Lotte, feeling the frightful state her words had thrust him into, tried by all manner of questions to divert his thoughts, but in vain.—'No, Lotte,' he cried, 'I shan't see you again.'—'Why so?' she answered, 'Werther, you can, you must see us again, only moderate your feelings. Oh why did you have to be born with this vehemence, this uncontrollable clinging passion for everything you ever touch? I beg you,' she continued, taking him by the hand, 'be more moderate. Your intelligence, your knowledge, your talents, what manifold enjoyments they offer you! Be a man! Turn this sad attachment away from a woman who can do no more than feel sorry for you.'—He ground his teeth and glowered at her. She held his hand. 'One moment's calm reflection, Werther,' she said. 'Can you not feel that you are deceiving yourself and with intention steering towards your ruin? Why me, Werther? Why precisely me, the property of another man? Why that precisely? I fear, I fear, it is only the impossibility of possessing me that makes this desire so exciting to you.'—He withdrew his hand from hers and the look he gave her was fixed and hostile.—'Clever,' he cried, 'very clever! Was it perhaps Albert who made the observation? Astute, very astute.'—'Anyone might make it,' she answered. 'And can there really be no other young woman in the whole wide world who would answer the desires of your heart? Force yourself, look for her, and I swear to you, you will find her. For a long time the narrowness of the life into which you have banished yourself here has made me fearful, for you and for us. Force yourself, travel will distract you, *must* distract you. Seek and find some worthy object of your love, and return here then and allow us to enjoy together the blissful happiness of a true friendship.'

'You might publish that,' he said with a cold laugh, 'and recommend it to every house-tutor. My dear Lotte, leave me in peace for a little while and what will be will be.'—'Only the one thing, Werther: that you won't come till Christmas Eve.'—He was about to answer, Albert entered the room. They exchanged a frosty 'Good evening' and walked up and down together in embarrassment. Werther began some idle topic, which soon came to nothing, Albert did the same and then asked his wife about certain matters and when he heard they had not yet been attended to he said words to her which Werther thought cold, indeed harsh. He wished to leave, couldn't, and delayed till eight, his unease and bad feelings increasing till the table was laid, when he took his hat and his stick. Albert invited him to stay but, thinking this an empty courtesy, he thanked him coldly, declined, and left.

He reached home and when the manservant came to light him in he took the lamp out of his hand and went alone into his room, wept aloud, talked wildly to himself, strode in much agitation up and down, and at last flung himself fully clothed on the bed where his servant, finally daring to enter towards eleven, found him and asked did the gentleman want his boots pulling off, which he allowed and told the servant not to come in next morning until he was called.

Monday morning early, 21 December, he began the letter to Lotte which was found sealed on his desk after his death and delivered to her and from which I shall quote passages at those points in the narrative when the circumstances seem to indicate they were written.

'It is decided, Lotte, I shall die and I write this to you* not in romantic fervour but calmly, on the morning of the day on which I shall see you for the last time. When you read this, my dearest, the cool grave will already house the stiffened remains of the restless and unhappy man who knows no sweeter thing for the last moments of his life than conversation with you. I have passed a terrible night—and oh, a beneficent night—a night that has made firm and definite my decision: I shall die. When I tore myself from you yesterday, in the frightful raging of my senses and everything assaulted my heart and my hopeless and joyless existence in your company seized hold of me, cruel and cold—I hardly reached my room, I was beside myself, went down on my knees, and there— God granted me the last relief of bitter, bitter tears. A thousand plans, a thousand prospects fought and clamoured through my soul, but one stood there at last, firmly and entirely, the last and only thought: I shall die.—I lay down and this morning in the calm of my waking still it stands there, still whole and strong in my heart: I shall die.—It is not despair, it is the certainty that I have suffered my fill and that I am sacrificing myself for you. Yes, Lotte, why should I not say it? One of the three of us must go and I will be the one. Oh my dearest, often through this lacerated heart of mine the thought has crept and raged—to murder your husband— you—myself! So be it then.—When you climb the hill on a lovely summer evening, remember me so often coming towards you up the valley, and then look across to the churchyard and to my grave

and see the wind in the glow of sunset waving the tall grasses to
and fro.—I was calm when I began but now, now I am weeping like
a child, all of that has come so much to life around me.—'

Towards ten o'clock Werther called his servant and whilst dressing
said to him that in a few days he was going on a journey so he
should brush his clothes and make everything ready to be packed.
He also ordered him to call in any bills, collect a few books he
had lent, and pay two months allowance in advance to a few poor
people he usually aided every week.

He had a meal brought to his room and having eaten it he rode
out to the Land Steward's but did not find him at home. In deep
thought he paced the garden seeking, as it seemed, to heap upon
himself all the sadness of memories at the last.

The children did not leave him in peace for long, they came
after him, leaped up at him, and said that after tomorrow and
another tomorrow and one more day after that they were going to
Lotte's for their Christmas presents and told him the wonders
their childish imaginations foretold.—'Tomorrow,' he cried, 'and
another tomorrow and one more day after that!'—and kissed them
all lovingly and made to leave.—But the youngest still had something to whisper in his ear—the secret that his big brothers had
written lovely New Year wishes, such big letters—one for Papa,
for Albert, for Lotte, and one for Herr Werther too. They would
present them early on the morning of New Year's Day. That overwhelmed him, he gave them all something, mounted his horse,
asked them to convey his best wishes to their father, and rode away
with tears in his eyes.

He came home towards five, told the maid to see to the fire and
to keep it burning into the night. He ordered his servant to pack
his books and linen first in the trunk and to sew up his clothes in
their wrappings. Probably after that he wrote the following paragraph of his last letter to Lotte.

'You are not expecting me, you think I will obey you and not see
you again till Christmas Eve. Oh Lotte, today or never again! On
Christmas Eve you will hold this paper in your trembling hand

and your sweet tears will water it. I will, I must! Oh, how it gladdens me that I have made up my mind.'

Lotte meanwhile had fallen into a peculiar state. After her last conversation with Werther she had felt how hard it would be for her to part from him and what he would suffer if he had to distance himself from her.

It had in passing been mentioned in Albert's presence that Werther would not come again before Christmas Eve, and Albert had ridden out to an official in the neighbourhood with whom he had some business to conclude and at whose house he would have to stay the night.

She sat alone, none of her brothers and sisters was around her, she gave herself up to her thoughts which moved in the silence here and there over her circumstances. She saw herself joined eternally to a man whose love and fidelity she knew, to whom she was deeply devoted, whose calm and reliability seemed sent by heaven to be the grounds on which a good woman could build her life's happiness, and she felt what he would always be to her and to her children. On the other hand, Werther had become so precious to her, from the moment they met the consonance of their spirits had been so beautifully apparent, the long time in his company, so many situations they had lived through together, had made an indelible impression on her heart. She had grown used to sharing everything interesting she ever felt and thought with him and his going threatened to tear a gap in her entire existence that would never be filled. Oh, if at that moment she could have changed him into a brother how happy she would have been!—or had she been free to marry him to one of her friends she might have hoped to restore his relationship with Albert wholly to what it was.

She had gone through all her women friends one by one and found something to object to in each. There wasn't one she would have let have him.

Through all this thinking she felt for the first time deeply, without quite making it explicit, that her passionate and secret desire was to keep him for herself; and alongside that she told herself that she could not, was not allowed to keep him. Her pure, lovely, and once so easy mind, a mind that had once so easily aided itself, now felt oppressed by the melancholy that comes when the prospect of happiness is closed off. Her heart was beset and her eyes were veiled in a darkness.

By now it was half-past six. She heard Werther coming up the steps, recognized his footfall, and then his voice asking after her. How her heart thumped—we might almost say for the first time— at his arrival. She would have wished he could be told she was not at home and when he entered she cried out to him in a sort of passionate confusion: 'You broke your promise!'—'I did not promise,' was his answer.—'Well at least you should have done what I asked,' she replied. 'I asked it for the peace of mind of us both.'

She hardly knew what she was saying, nor what she was doing when she sent out to a couple of her women friends so as not to be alone with Werther. He laid down some books he had brought, enquired about some others, and she wished now that her friends would come, now that they wouldn't. The girl came back to say that both sent their apologies.

She thought of having the girl sit with her work in the adjoining room; then changed her mind. Werther paced to and fro, she went to the piano and began a minuet, but it faltered. She pulled herself together and sat down composedly by Werther who had seated himself as usual on the sofa.

'Have you nothing you might read?' she said.—He had nothing.—'Over there in my drawer', she began, 'is your translation of some of the poems of Ossian.* I haven't read them yet, I always hoped to hear you read them, but all this time it hasn't happened, we haven't managed it.'—He smiled, fetched the songs, a shudder went through him as he took them in his hands and his eyes filled with tears when he looked at them. He sat down again and read.

'Star of the coming night, you sparkle in beauty in the west, you lift your head clear of the cloud, arrayed, and down the hillside you proceed in majesty. What are you looking for across the moors? The storming winds have ceased, there is a distant murmuring of streams and around the distant cliffs the waves are moving, there is an evening hum of insects over the fields. Beautiful light, what are you looking for? But you smile and depart, joyfully your waves surround you and bathe your lovely hair. Farewell, calm radiance. Appear now in your splendour, light of Ossian's soul!

'And in its strength that light appears. I see my departed friends, they gather on Lora as in the days that are gone.—Fingal comes like a watery column of mist, his heroes are around him and see— the bards, grey Ullin, stately Ryno, Alpin, the sweet singer, and you, Minona with your gentle laments!—How changed you are, my friends, since the festive days on Selma when we vied with one another for the glory of song. We were like the airs of spring that on the hillside turn by turn make a faint whispering through the bowing grass.

'Then in her beauty Minona stepped forward, her tearful eyes cast down, her hair lifting heavily in the wind that gusted from the hills.—There was darkness in the souls of the heroes when her sweet voice began. For they had often seen Salgar's grave and often white Colma's dark home. Colma with her melodious voice, forsaken on the hills. Salgar promised to come but the night closed all around her. Hear Colma's voice when she sat alone on the hills.

COLMA

'It is night, I am alone and forsaken on the stormy hills. The wind moans in the mountains, the river howls from the rocks. I have no hut for shelter from the rain, I am forsaken on the stormy hill.

'Moon, step forth from your clouds. Appear, stars of the night. Oh, let some radiance lead me to where my love lies resting from the labour of the hunt, his bow unstrung beside him and his hounds snuffling round. But I must sit alone on rocks above the swollen river. The river roars, the storm-wind roars, but I do not hear the voice of my beloved.

'Why does my Salgar tarry? Has he forgotten his promise?— Here are the rocks, the tree, the tumultuous river. You promised to be here at nightfall, oh where have you wandered to, my Salgar?

I was to flee with you and leave my proud father and brother. Our clans have long been enemies, but we are not enemies, Salgar.

'Wind, be silent for a while. River, be quiet for a little while so my voice may sound through the valley and my wanderer hear me. I am the voice calling you, Salgar. Here is the tree, here is the rock. Salgar, my love, I am here, why do you not come?

'See, the moon appears, the waters gleam in the valley, the rocks stand grey on the hillside, but I do not see him on the heights, his hounds ahead of him do not announce his coming. I must sit here alone.

'But who are they lying there below on the heather?—My beloved? My brother?—Speak, friends. They do not answer. My soul is sore afraid.—Oh they are dead, their swords are red from the combat. Brother, oh my brother, why have you killed Salgar? Oh Salgar, why have you killed my brother? You were both so dear to me. Oh, you were lovely among thousands on the hills. He was fearsome in battle. Answer me, hear my voice, oh my dear ones. But they are dumb, for all eternity dumb, cold as the earth is the heart of each in his body.

'Oh from the hill's rocks, from the storm peaks of the mountains, speak, ghosts of the dead, speak, I will not shudder at it.—Where have you gone to your rest? In what vault of the mountains am I to find you?—I hear no faint voice in the wind, no answer blows towards me in the blast around the hill.

'I sit in my sorrow, I wait for morning in my tears. Gouge out a grave, O you friends of the dead, but do not close it till I come. My life is vanishing like a dream, how should I remain behind? I will live here with my friends by the river and the sounding rocks.— When night falls over the hill and the wind comes over the heather my ghost will stand in the wind and bewail the deaths of my friends. The hunter in his greenery will hear me, he will fear my voice and he will love it, for my voice will be sweet in the song over my friends, for both were dear to me.

'That was your song, Minona, softly blushing daughter of Torman. Our tears flowed for Colma and darkness came over our souls.

'Ullin stepped up with the harp and gave us the song of Alpin.—Alpin's voice was kind, Ryno's soul a blaze of light. But they lay already in the narrow home and their voices had faded out of Selma. Once Ullin was returning from the hunt at a time before the heroes had fallen. He heard them on the hill competing in song. Their song was gentle but sad. They lamented the fall of Morar, first of the heroes. His soul was like Fingal's soul, his sword like the sword of Oscar.—But he fell and his father sorrowed and his sister's eyes were full of tears, Minona the sister of lordly Morar, her eyes were full of tears. She withdrew when Ullin began his song as the moon does in the west when she sees the rainstorm coming and hides her lovely head in cloud.—I struck the harp with Ullin for the song of sorrow.

RYNO

'The wind and the rain have passed over, noon is fair, the clouds open. Fleetingly the restless sun lights up the hill. The mountain river coursing down the valley has a reddish look. River, your murmuring is sweet but the voice I hear is sweeter. It is the voice of Alpin bewailing the dead man. His head is bowed with age and his eyes are red with weeping. Alpin, excellent singer, why are you alone on the speechless hill, why do you lament like a wind among trees, like waves upon a distant shore?

ALPIN

'My tears, Ryno, are for the man who is dead, my voice for the dwellers in graves. You are tall and slim on the hill, you are pleasing to look at among the sons of the heath. But you will fall like Morar and one will sit lamenting over your grave. The hills will forget you, your bow will lie unstrung in the great hall.

'Morar, you were swift as the deer on the hills, terrible as the fires of night upon the sky. Your anger was a tempest, your sword in the battle was like sheet lightning over the heather. Your voice was like a woodland torrent after rain or thunder on the far hills. Many fell by the force of your arm, the flames of your rage consumed them. But when you returned from warfare how peaceful was your brow, your countenance was like the sea after the thunderstorm, like the moon in the silence of night, and your breast was as quiet as the lake when the rushing winds have ceased.

'Now your house is a narrow one, it is dark where you dwell. I measure your grave in three paces, you who once were great. Four stones with mossy heads are your only memorial, a leafless tree, long grass that whispers in the wind mark for the hunter the grave of Morar. You have no mother to weep and no girl either with the tears of love. The woman who bore you is dead, the daughter of Morglan is fallen.

'Who leans there on his staff? Who is that whose head is white with age and the eyes in it red with tears? It is your father, Morar, the father of no other son but you. He heard of your fame in battle, he heard of your enemies scattered like dust, he heard of the glory of Morar—but nothing of his wound? Weep, you may weep, father of Morar, but your son will not hear you. The sleep of the dead is deep, sunk on a pillow of dust. He will never hearken to your voice, he will never wake when you cry out. Oh, when will day break in the grave and bid the sleeper wake?

'Farewell, noblest of men, victor on the battlefield. The field will never see you now, never will the dark woods light up with the gleam of your steel. You left no son, let song preserve your name, future ages will hear of you, they will hear of Morar who has fallen.

'The heroes' grief was loud, loudest were the sighs of Armin as though his heart would burst. It had caused him to remember the death of his son who fell in the days of his youth. Carmor, prince of echoing Galmal, sat close by the hero. "What sobbing and sighing is this of Armin's?" he asked. "What is there to bewail? Do we not have songs and hymns that melt and refresh the soul? They are like a soft mist that rises from the lake and moisture fills the flowers and they bloom. But the sun comes again in his strength and the mists depart. Why are you so sorrowful, Armin, ruler of Gorma among the waves?"

'Sorrowful indeed I am and my grief has a heavy cause.

—Carmor, you have not lost a son, you have not lost a daughter in the flower of her beauty. Brave Colgar lives and Annira, the loveliest of young women. The branches of your house are thriving, Carmor, but Armin is the last of his clan. Daura, your bed is a dark place, your sleep in the grave is heavy. When will you wake with your songs and your sweet voice? Let the winds of autumn rise and come in storms over the black moors! Let the torrent roar through the forest and the tempest howl in the crowns of the oaks and the moon show her changing face in pallor through the breaking cloud—so that I will remember the night of horror in which my children died, mighty Arindal falling and Daura, my dear one, going from me.

'Daura, my daughter, you were beautiful as the moon on the hills of Fura, white as the fallen snow, sweet as the breathing air. Arindal, your bow was strong, your spear quick in the field, your eyes like mist on the waves, your shield a cloud of fire in the stormwind.

'Armar, famous in warfare, came wooing Daura for her love. She did not withhold it long and the hopes of their friends were high.

'Erath, son of Odgal, was not content. His brother lay dead by the hand of Armar. He came disguised as a boatman. His craft was beautiful on the waves, his hair white with age, his face solemn. Loveliest of women, he said, sweet daughter of Armin, there on the rocky island, not far off shore, where the red berries shine in that tree, Armar waits for Daura. I have come to ferry his love across the rolling sea.

'She went with him and called for Armar. Nothing answered but the voice of the rocks. Armar, my love, why do you frighten me so? Hear me, son of Armar, hear me—it is Daura calling for you.

'The treacherous Erath fled laughing to the shore. She raised her voice, calling for her father and her brother, Arindal! Armar! Is there no one who will rescue Daura?

'Her voice came over the sea. Arindal, my son, climbed down the hill, fierce with the spoils of the hunt, his arrows rattling on his hip, his bow was in his hand, five dark grey hounds were about him. He saw bold Erath on the shore, seized and bound him to the oak tree, fastened him tight about the hips, and Erath in his bondage freighted the winds with his groans.

'Arindal trod the waves with his boat to fetch Daura across. Armar came in his rage, loosed the grey-flighted arrow, it howled through the air into your heart, Arindal, oh my son! It was you who died, not the treacherous Erath. The boat reached the island rocks, there he sank down and died. Your brother's blood flowed at your feet. What grief was yours, Daura!

'The waves smashed the boat. Armar leapt into the sea, to save Daura or die. A great turbulence rushed off the hills into the waters. He sank and did not rise again.

'I heard the crying of my daughter alone on the sea-washed rocks. Her cries were many and loud but her father could not save her. I stood all night on the shore, I saw her in the faint moonlight, all night I heard her crying, the wind was loud, the rain struck slant and sharp against the cliff. Her voice grew weak, she faded into death before morning came, she died like the evening air among the grasses and the rocks. She died laden with grief and left Armin alone. My tower of strength in the wars is fallen, my pride and joy among the young women is no more.

'When the storms of the mountains come, when the north wind lifts the waves high, I sit on the echoing shore and look across to the fearful rocks. Often under the declining moon I see the ghosts of my children. In a dimming light they walk together in sad companionship.'

A sudden release of Lotte's feelings in a rush of tears halted Werther's reading of these songs. He flung the sheets down, seized her hand, and wept most bitterly. Lotte rested on the other hand and hid her eyes in her handkerchief. In her and in Werther the agitation of feeling was terrible. They felt their own wretchedness in the fates of those noble persons, felt it together and their tears united them. Werther's lips and eyes were on Lotte's arm, they burned, a cold shudder went through her, she wished to move away and pain and fellow-feeling lay upon her so that she was drugged and leaden. She drew breath, to recover herself and, still sobbing, begged him to continue, entreated him with heaven's own power of speech. Werther trembled, he felt his heart would burst, he lifted up the page and read, half-brokenly:

'Why wake me, airs of spring?* You cajole me, saying, I water with the dew of heaven. But the time of my withering is near, the tempest is near that will dash down my leaves. Tomorrow the traveller will come who saw me in my beauty, he will seek me all around in the fields and will not find me.—'

These words came over the unhappy man with all their force. In utter despair he flung himself down before Lotte, seized her hands, pressed them into his eyes and against his forehead, and a presentiment of his terrible intention seemed to flit through her soul. Her senses were confused, she squeezed his hands, pressed them to her heart, bowed sorrowfully over him, and their cheeks touched, burning. The world was lost to them. He clasped her in his arms, pressed her to his heart, and overwhelmed her trembling and stammering lips with a rage of kisses.—'Werther!' she cried, her voice choked, averting her face, 'Werther!'—and with a weak hand she pushed his breast from hers.—'Werther!' she cried in the determined tones of a noble sentiment.—He did not resist, he let her out of his arms and threw himself down before her in a frenzy. She got hastily to her feet and in fearful confusion, shaken between love and anger, she said: 'That is the last time, Werther! You will not see me again.'— And with a look all full of love at him in his misery she hurried into the adjoining room and locked the door behind her. Werther stretched out his arms after her, not having dared to hold her back. He lay on the floor with his head on the sofa and stayed in that position more than half an hour, until a noise called him back to himself. It was the servant girl wanting to set the table. He paced the room and when he was alone again he went to the door and called in a low voice, 'Lotte, Lotte, only one word more.—A goodbye.'—She said nothing, he waited, begged her again, waited. Then he tore himself away, crying, 'Goodbye, Lotte! Goodbye for ever!'

He came to the town gates. The watchmen, who were used to him, said nothing and let him out. It was sleeting thinly. Not till eleven did he knock to come in again. When Werther reached home the servant noticed that his master's hat was missing. He didn't dare make any comment; undressed him, everything was wet. Afterwards his hat was found on a rock overlooking the valley from the hillside and how he had climbed up there on a dark wet night without falling is unimaginable.

He went to bed and slept for a long time. The servant found him writing when, summoned the next morning, he brought him his coffee. He added the following to his letter to Lotte:

'So for the last time I open these eyes, for the last time. Oh, they shan't see the sun any more, a dull and foggy day obscures it. Grieve then, Nature: your son, your friend, your beloved, is nearing his end. Lotte, it is a feeling like no other, but what it most resembles is a twilit dream, to say to oneself: this morning is the last. The last! Lotte, the word makes no sense to me—the last! Do I not stand here in all my strength? And tomorrow I lie slack upon the floor. To die—what does it mean? Surely we are dreaming when we speak of death. I have seen more than one person die, but human beings are so limited they have no sense or understanding of the beginning and end of their existences. Now still mine, yours—yours, my beloved! And then in a moment—parted, sundered—perhaps for ever?—No, Lotte, no—How can I cease to be? How can you cease to be? We *are!*—Cease to be!—What does it mean? More words, empty sounds, my heart cannot feel them.——Dead, Lotte, dug into the cold earth, so cramped, so dark!—I had a friend, in my helpless youth she was everything to me, she died and I followed her corpse and stood at the grave as they lowered the coffin and the ropes hustled down beneath it and hurried back up again and the first shovelful of earth thudded down and the fearful box resounded dully and ever more dully until at last it was covered.—I prostrated myself at the graveside—into the innermost part of me seized, shaken, terrified, and torn, but all without comprehending what was happening to me—what will happen to me.—To die! The grave! I don't understand the words.

'Oh forgive me, forgive me! Yesterday, it ought to have been the last moment of my life. Oh, you angel, for the first time, for the first time quite beyond any doubt, it burned through the innermost heart of me, the blissful feeling: she loves me! She loves me! On my lips still burns the sacred fire that flowed from yours, a warm, new bliss is in my heart. Forgive me! Forgive me!

'Oh, I knew you loved me, knew it from the first soulful looks, the first pressure of your hand, but when I was away from you again, when I saw Albert at your side, I despaired again in a feverish doubting.

'Do you remember the flowers you sent me after that tiresome gathering when you couldn't speak to me at all or give me your hand? Oh, I knelt before them half the night and they were for me the seal upon your love. But those impressions also passed just as the feeling of the grace of the god he worships, given him in heaven's entire abundance in holy and visible signs, gradually lapses out of the believer's soul.

'All such things pass but an eternity will not extinguish the burning life that I took into me yesterday from off your lips and feel in me still. She loves me! These arms of mine enfolded her, these lips trembled on her lips, this mouth stammered on hers. She is mine, you are mine, yes, Lotte, for ever.

'And what does it matter that Albert is your husband? Husband! That may be so for this world—and for this world a sin that I love you and should like to tear you out of his arms and into mine. A sin? Very well, and I am punishing myself for it. I have tasted this sin in all its heavenly bliss and sucked the balm and power of life in it into my heart. From this moment on you are mine, Lotte, mine. I go ahead, to my Father,* to your Father. I will make my complaint to Him and He will comfort me until you come and I will fly to you and have hold of you and be with you in His everlasting sight in eternal embraces.

'I am not dreaming, I am not deluded, close to the grave I see more clearly. We shall not pass away, we shall see one another again. See your mother, I shall see your mother, I shall seek and find her and pour out all my heart before her. Your mother, the image of you!'

Towards eleven Werther asked his servant whether Albert was back. His servant answered yes, he had seen his horse being led in. Thereupon his master gave him the following unsealed note:*

'Would you mind lending me your pistols for a journey I intend to take? Sincere good wishes. Farewell.'

Poor Lotte had slept very little. What she had feared was now decided—decided in a way she could not have suspected or feared. She, whose natural temperament was so clear and bright, now felt a fever and an upheaval in her blood; her inner grace was assailed and shaken by a thousand different feelings. Was it the passion of Werther's embraces that she felt in her breast? Was it anger at his effrontery? Was it the sadness of comparing her present state with those days of free and wholly untroubled innocence and careless trust in herself? How should she face her husband? How admit to him a scene she had no reason to hide but yet did not dare confess? They had been silent with one another so long and must she be the one to break that silence and at quite the wrong moment make such an unexpected disclosure to her husband? She was afraid that even to learn of Werther's visit would affect him disagreeably— and now this unexpected catastrophe! Could she really hope that her husband would view it entirely in the right light and hear her quite without prejudice? And could she wish that he might read in her soul? On the other hand, how could she dissemble with a man before whom she had always stood as clear and transparent as a bright crystal glass and from whom she had never concealed and never would be able to conceal any of her feelings? One thing and another troubled and embarrassed her, and always her thoughts returned to Werther who was lost for her, whom she could not let go and whom, alas, she must leave to himself and who, losing her, had nothing left.

How heavily—though at that moment she could not see it—the constraint lay upon her which had settled between the two of them. Good and sensible people had, because of certain secret differences, ceased to talk to one another, each brooded on their own rightness and the other's wrongness and things became so fraught and complicated that at precisely the critical moment on which all depended it was impossible to untie the knot. Had they before now by some happy intimacy been brought close again, had a mutual love and understanding come alive between them and opened their hearts, perhaps our friend might still have been saved.

There was a further strange circumstance. As we know from his letters, Werther had never made any secret of the fact that he longed to leave the world. Albert had often argued with him about it and between husband and wife it had also more than once been discussed. Albert, who felt a decided revulsion towards such an act, had moreover, with a quite uncharacteristic irritability, intimated that there were strong grounds for doubting the seriousness of Werther's intention, had even gone so far as to joke about it and had communicated his scepticism to Lotte. On the one hand she was reassured by this whenever her thoughts led her to contemplate the sad prospect; on the other, it inhibited her from sharing with her husband the anxieties presently tormenting her.

Albert came back and Lotte hurried in embarrassment to meet him. He was not in a good humour, his business had not been concluded, he had found the local official to be obdurate and small-minded. The bad roads had further annoyed him.

He asked had anything happened, and hastily she answered that Werther had been there the evening before. He asked were there any letters, and her answer was that a letter and some packages were in his study. He went in, leaving Lotte alone. The presence of the man she loved and honoured had made a new impression on her heart. Remembering his magnanimity, his love and kindness, calmed her mind, she felt drawn to follow him, she took her work and went into his room as she often did. She found him busy opening and reading the packages. The contents of some seemed not to be very agreeable. She asked him one or two questions, which he answered curtly and moved to his desk to write.

They were together in this fashion for an hour and the darkness deepened in Lotte's spirit. She felt how difficult it would be to divulge to her husband, even had he been in the best of moods, what weighed on her heart. She fell into a sadness that became all the more distressing as she strove to hide it and to choke back her tears.

Werther's servant appeared, to her utmost consternation. He handed Albert the note. Albert turned calmly to Lotte and said: 'Give him the pistols.'—Then, addressing the youth, he said, 'I wish him a safe journey.'—That struck her like a thunderbolt, she rose very unsteadily to her feet, not knowing what she was doing. Slowly she went to the wall, trembling took down the guns, dusted them, and hesitated and would have hesitated longer had not Albert with a questioning look urged her on. She gave the unhappy implements to the servant without being able to utter a word and when he had left the house she gathered up her work and went to her own room in an anxiety beyond expression. Her heart foretold her all manner of horrors. She was on the verge of throwing herself at her husband's feet and confessing everything to him, the whole story of the previous evening, her guilt and her bad presentiments. But what would such a move achieve? Least likely was that she would be able to persuade him to go and see Werther. The table was laid and a good friend, only come to ask something and about to leave, stayed and made the conversation over the meal bearable; they forced themselves, they talked, they recounted things, they forgot themselves.

The servant came with the pistols to Werther, who received them in an ecstasy when he heard that Lotte had given them to him. He had bread and wine brought, sent the young man off to eat, sat down, and wrote:

'They have passed through your hands, you wiped the dust off them, I kiss them a thousand times, you touched them. The spirits of heaven favour my decision! And you, Lotte, you hand me the instruments, you from whose hands I desired to receive my death and now receive it! Oh I questioned my boy very closely! You trembled when you handed them to him, you said no goodbye— Oh alas, alas, no farewell!—Am I to think you have closed your heart against me on account of the one moment that bound me to you for ever? Lotte, a thousand years will not erase the imprint and I feel that you cannot hate the man who burns for you as I do.'

Having eaten, he ordered his servant to finish the packing, tore up a great many papers, went out and settled a few small debts. He came home, went out again, outside the town gates, in the Count's park, despite the rain wandered further thereabouts, and at nightfall returned and wrote:

'Wilhelm, I have looked for the last time on the fields, the woods and the sky. To you also now I say farewell. My dear mother, forgive me. Comfort her, Wilhelm. God bless you both. My affairs are all in order. Farewell, we shall meet again and be happier.'

'You have had a poor reward from me, Albert—you will forgive me. I have disturbed the peace of your house and brought mistrust between you. Farewell, I will end it. Oh may you be happy by my death! Albert, Albert, make her, the angel, happy. And so may God's blessing abide with you.'

In the evening he did a good deal more sorting through his papers, tore up many of them and flung them in the stove, sealed up some packets and addressed them to Wilhelm. They contained short essays, stray thoughts, various of which I have seen. And having around ten had the fire made up and a bottle of wine fetched, he sent the servant to bed. The servant's room as well as the sleeping quarters of the landlord and his family were some distance behind the house. The servant lay down in his clothes to be on hand early next morning because his master had said the post-horses would be there before six.

After 11

Everything is so still all around me and my soul so quiet. Thanks be to God that He has granted me this warmth, this strength, in these my last moments.

I step to the window, my dearest, and through the hastening storm-clouds I see, I still see, a few single stars of the eternal heavens. No, you will never fall—the everlasting God holds you in His heart as He holds me. I see the stars that make the shaft of the Plough, dearest to me among all the constellations. When I left you at night, when I stepped out through your gate, there it stood before me and over me. Oh, often and in such elation I gazed on it, raised my hands towards it to be the sign, the sacred marker of the bliss that was present in me then! And also—oh, Lotte, is there anything that doesn't remind me of you? Do you not encompass me all around? Like a child, never satisfied, I clutched every little thing to me that you, my icon, had ever touched.

Dear silhouette. I bequeathe it back to you, Lotte, and beg you to honour it. Many thousand kisses I have pressed upon it, saluted it a thousand times at my going out and at my coming in.

I have written a note to your father asking him to give my body his protection. In the graveyard there are two lime trees, at the back in the corner, towards the field: I should like to lie there. He can and will do that for his friend. You ask him too. I wouldn't want good Christian folk to have to lay their bodies down beside a poor unfortunate. Oh I wish you'd bury me by the wayside or in a lonely valley so the priest and the Levite could pass by the marked stone and ask a blessing upon themselves and the Samaritan* shed a tear.

Here, Lotte, without a shudder I take up the cold and fearful cup* from which I am to drink intoxicating death. You handed it to me and I am not afraid. All, all! This then is the fulfilment of all my life's hopes and desires. So cold, so frozenly to knock at the brazen gates of death.

If only I could have had the happiness of dying for you, Lotte, of sacrificing myself for you. I would die bravely, I would die joy-fully, if I could give your life its peace and its delight again. But alas, it is given to only a few of the noblest to spill their blood for their loved ones and to quicken by their death new life for their friends a hundredfold.

Lotte, I want to be buried in these clothes, you have touched them and thereby made them holy. I asked that of your father too. My soul hovers over the coffin. Let nobody search my pockets. This pale-red ribbon which you had on your bosom the first time I came upon you among your children—oh, kiss them a thousand times and tell them about the fate of their unhappy friend. My dear ones! They jostle around me. Oh how I cleaved to you, from that first moment could not let you go!—This ribbon is to be bur-ied with me. It was your present to me on my birthday. How I devoured all that!—Oh I never thought the way would lead me here.——Be at peace, I beg you, be at peace.—

They are loaded—It is striking twelve. So be it then.—Lotte, Lotte, farewell, farewell.

A neighbour saw the powder flash and heard the shot. But then, since all was quiet he gave no further thought to it.

Next morning at six the servant went in with a light. He found his master on the floor, the pistol, blood. He shouted, he grasped him—no answer, there was only the rattle in his throat. He ran for a doctor, for Albert. Lotte heard the bell pulled, all her limbs were taken with a trembling. She woke her husband, they got up, the servant, stammering and crying, gave them the news. Lotte fell unconscious at Albert's feet.

When the doctor reached the unfortunate man he found him on the floor beyond saving, the pulse still beating, his limbs all lamed. He had shot himself through the head above the right eye, blowing his brains out. They opened a vein in his arm, the blood flowed, he was still drawing breath.

It could be deduced from the blood on the back of the chair that he had carried out the act sitting at his desk, then slid down and rolled in convulsions around the chair. He lay on his back, towards the window, all the strength gone out of him, fully clothed, with his boots on, in the blue frock-coat and buff-yellow waistcoat.

The house, the neighbourhood, the town were in a commotion. Albert came in. They had laid Werther on the bed, his forehead bound up, his face already like that of a dead man, he made no movement. There was still a terrible rattling in his lungs, now weaker, now stronger. They awaited his end.

Of the wine he had only drunk one glass. *Emilia Galotti** lay open on the desk

Dispense me from saying anything of Albert's dismay and Lotte's desolation.

The old Land Steward came post-haste at the news, he kissed the dying man in a passion of weeping. His eldest sons followed soon after on foot, they fell down by his bed, quite at the mercy of their grief, they kissed his hands, his mouth, and the eldest, whom he had always loved best,* hung on his lips until he passed away and they dragged the boy off him by force. He died at twelve noon. The presence of the Land Steward and the measures he took hushed up any public outcry. At night towards eleven he had him buried in the place he had chosen for himself. The old man followed the coffin with his sons, Albert could not do it. They feared for Lotte's life. Working-men carried him. No priest attended.

EXPLANATORY NOTES

5 *Poor Leonore!*: Goethe got into a similar entanglement in Strasburg with the daughters of his dancing-master and describes it in Book 9 of *Dichtung und Wahrheit*.

my aunt: Goethe had a great-aunt in Wetzlar.

6 *Count M.*: a certain Procurator Meckel had a large garden on the slopes of the Lahnberg outside Wetzlar laid out in the English (informal and natural) style—which Werther much prefers to the French.

7 *there is a well*: there was such a spring or well by the Wildbacher Tor, on the way out of Wetzlar towards Count M.'s garden. After *Werther* it became known as the *Goethebrunnen*.

Melusina: in European folklore, a water sprite or mermaid. A version of her legend by the fourteenth-century French writer Jean d'Arras was widely translated.

courtships would begin: see Genesis 24: 13 ff., Abraham's servant and Rebekah; also Genesis 29, Jacob and Rachel.

Homer: in the 1770s Goethe admired Homer as Werther does, for his vigour and naturalness, against the complexity and artificiality of modern manners.

9 *the friend of my youth*: Werther mentions her again in his final letter to Lotte (p. 104). She may be an after-image of the Pietist Susanne von Klettenberg, who was a sentimental mentor to Goethe in Frankfurt, 1768–70.

10 *Batteux . . . Wood . . . de Piles . . . Winckelmann*: Charles Batteux (1713–80), author of *Cours de belles lettres ou Principes de la littérature* (1747–50). Robert Wood (1716–71), author of *An Essay on the Original Genius of Homer*. A first version of this important work was thoroughly reviewed and so made known in Germany by Heyne (see below) in March 1770. The book appeared in German in 1773. Goethe acknowledged its influence on his thinking. Roger de Piles (1635–1709), author of several theoretical works on painting. Johann Joachim Winckelmann (1717–68), the hugely influential author of, among much else, *Gedanken über die Nachahmung der griechischen Werke* (*Thoughts upon the Imitation of Greek Works*, 1755) and *Geschichte der Kunst des Altertums* (*History of Ancient Art*, 1764). He was murdered in Trieste. Like Wood, Winckelmann was of considerable importance to Goethe. In his essay 'Winckelmann und sein Jahrhundert' (1805), Goethe called Winckelmann's scholarship 'something living for the living and not for those entombed in the dead letter'.

Sulzer's Theory: Johann Georg Sulzer (1720–79), author of *Allgemeine Theorie der Schönen Künste* (*General Theory of the Fine Arts*), the first part of which appeared in 1771.

10 *Heyne*: Christian Gottlob Heyne (1729–1812), Professor of Classical Philology at the University of Göttingen, another authority whom Goethe gratefully acknowledged.

Duke's Land Steward: Goethe had Heinrich Adam Buff in mind, father of Charlotte.

11 *this prison*: Werther will return to and expand on this motif. Goethe doubtless had *Hamlet*, II. ii in mind: 'HAMLET: Denmark's a prison. | ROSENCRANTZ: Then is the world one.' He had already alluded to that exchange in the final scene of his *Götz von Berlichingen*.

Wahlheim: usually thought to be Garbenheim, a couple of miles east of Wetzlar.

14 *30 May*: this letter was added when Goethe revised *Werther* for publication in 1787.

16 *a dance*: Goethe met Charlotte Sophie Henriette Buff (1753–1828) at a dance on 9 June 1772 at Volpertshausen, just south of Wetzlar.

17 *Charlotte S.*: see above and Introduction.

the most charming spectacle: engraved as an illustration in some editions of *Werther* and comically celebrated by Thackeray in his poem 'Sorrows of Werther'.

19 *Miss Jenny*: a typical heroine of contemporary romantic novels for which, after Richardson, England was a popular setting. Marie-Jeanne Riccoboni (1714–92), for example, wrote a *Histoire de Miss Jenny Glanville* which was translated into German in 1764.

The Vicar of Wakefield: novel by Oliver Goldsmith, published in 1766; a German translation, by J. G. Gellius, was published in Leipzig in 1767. Herder read it aloud to Goethe and other visitors in the winter of 1770–1. In *Dichtung und Wahrheit* Goethe's account of his love affair with the daughter of a rural pastor, Friederike Brion, is rather in the style of *The Vicar of Wakefield*.

20 *anglaise*: English country dance.

allemande: a form of country dance (*contredanse*) involving a waltz.

23 *Klopstock . . . wonderful ode*: Friedrich Gottlob Klopstock (1724–1803), author of *Messias* (from 1748) and of much lyric poetry treating love, friendship, religion, and nature. The ode Lotte and Werther remember together is his 'Frühlingsfeier' ('Festival of Spring') of 1759.

25 *the suitors*: the suitors for the hand of Penelope in Odysseus' absence; see e.g. *Odyssey* 2.300 ff. and 20.248 ff. Werther's allusions are not always quite apt.

26 *unless ye become as one of these*: refers to Matthew 18: 1–6.

Karlsbad: a spa in southern Germany, often visited by Goethe, first in the summer of 1785; it was from there, having finished the revision of *Werther*, that he fled to Italy in 1786.

27 *Friederike*: she shares the name with another daughter of a rural pastor, Friederike Brion. See the note on *The Vicar of Wakefield* above.

28 *Lavater*: Johann Caspar Lavater (1741–1801), a pietistic and enthusiastic theologian with an interest in physiognomy. The collection of sermons referred to here was published in 1773. See also p. 72.

30 *Malchen*: Charlotte Buff's youngest sister was called Amalie; Malchen is a diminutive of that name.

32 *Ossian*: see notes to pp. 73, 96, and 103.

the prophet's unfailing cruse of oil: see 1 Kings 17: 16. A cruse is an earthenware pot or jar.

33 *Loves me! . . . she loves me*: this paragraph was added in the revision.

34 *Bologna stone*: a phosphorescent form of barite (barium sulphate) first found near Bologna in the seventeenth century.

the Envoy: see note to p. 53.

35 *26 July*: added in revision before the following letter of the same date.

36 *the Magnetic Mountain*: in the *Arabian Nights* ('Tale of the Third Calender'), Prince Agib's ship falls to pieces when driven by the wind towards the mountain.

38 *Evening*: this paragraph on Werther's diary was added in revision.

40 *cast the first stone*: see John 8: 7.

41 *pass by like the priest . . . Pharisee*: see Luke 10: 31 and Luke 18: 11.

42 *sickness unto death*: see John 11: 4.

a girl who only recently had been found drowned: Goethe perhaps alludes to Anna Elisabeth Stöber, who drowned herself when her lover left her on 29 December 1769. She prefigures Christel von Lassberg; see Introduction, p. xxvii.

44 *the princess who was waited on by hands*: see the story 'La Chatte blanche' in the *Contes de fées* of Marie de Berneville, Countess of Aulnoy (?1650–1705).

47 *the fable of the horse*: see Horace, *Epistles* I. 10 and La Fontaine, *Fables*, IV. 13.

Today is my birthday: Goethe and Kestner had the same birthday: 28 August.

the pale-red ribbons: Charlotte Buff gave Goethe a bow she had worn at the ball in Volpertshausen where they met.

Wetstein . . . Ernesti: J. H. Wetstein published this duodecimo edition of Homer in Amsterdam in 1707—much handier than the edition in octavo published by J. A. Ernesti in Leipzig, 1759–64.

49 *10 September*: Goethe left Wetzlar abruptly on 11 September, having had a conversation with Kestner and Charlotte Buff similar to the one described in this letter. His farewell letter to Charlotte is dated 10 September.

53 *The Envoy*: for this character Goethe had in mind the Envoy of Brunswick, von Hoefler, the employer of Karl Wilhelm Jerusalem on whose unhappy life much of Book Two of *Werther* is based. See Introduction, pp. ix–x and xxviii.

54 *Count C.*: in Jerusalem's life-story this was a Count Bassenheim, who was kind to him but at whose house he suffered a humiliation such as Werther suffers.

56 *Fräulein von B.*: her real-life equivalent may be Luise von Ziegler (1750–1814), whom Goethe met in Darmstadt at the end of February 1772. She was said to suffer at Court rather as Fräulein von B. does.

Age of Bronze . . . Age of Iron: stages in some Classical schemes—the first in Hesiod's *Works and Days*—that chart the decline of the human condition.

57 *In the evening . . . is gone*: added in revision.

58 *8 February*: all of this letter was added in revision.

59 *20 February*: much of this letter is close to what Goethe wrote to Kestner on learning that he and Charlotte Buff had married.

60 *coronation of Franz I*: Franz was crowned Emperor in 1745.

appearing as Herr von R.: he appears at this gathering as a nobleman, not in his civic capacity of Privy Counsellor.

61 *read in my Homer . . . swineherd*: in Book 14 of the *Odyssey*, Odysseus, returning to Ithaca disguised as a beggar, is given hospitality by his old swineherd, Eumaeus.

65 *He has strange people . . . I can't trust them*: added in revision.

66 *16 June*: added in revision.

68 *4 September*: added in revision.

70 *5 September*: added in revision.

71 *12 September*: added in revision.

72 *Pastor's wife*: in characterizing her, Goethe may have had in mind the Pietist Dorothea Griesbach (1726–75), whom he had met in Frankfurt in the circle of Susanne von Klettenberg and remembered in Book 8 of *Dichtung und Wahrheit* as seeming 'too severe, too dry, too learned'.

fashionable moral-critical way: a tendency in contemporary theology, in C. F. Bahrdt (1741–92), for example, and J. B. Basedow (1723–90), to rationalize and secularize the person and the teachings of Christ.

Kennicott, Semler, and Michaelis: Benjamin Kennicott (1718–83), an English theologian, and Johann Salomo Semler (1725–91), Professor of Theology at Halle, were eminent in an Enlightenment movement that subjected the Bible to the textual and historical criticism long practised in Classical studies. Johann David Michaelis (1717–91), Professor of Oriental Languages at Göttingen and colleague of C. G. Heyne (see note to p. 10), supported that transference of knowledge and methodology. Lavater (see note to p. 27) represented an entirely opposite tendency: apprehension of the Bible through enthusiastic feeling.

73 *Ossian has displaced Homer in my heart*: Goethe commented to Henry Crabb Robinson in 1829 that 'Werther praised Homer while he retained his senses, and Ossian when he was going mad'. In 1760 James Macpherson (1736–96) published *Fragments of Ancient Poetry collected in the Highlands of Scotland*, attributing them to Ossian, a legendary Gaelic warrior-bard. This short first collection was the most closely based on the fluid oral originals that Macpherson heard throughout his childhood, and which he collected as a student; the subsequent 'epics' that rapidly grew out of them, *Fingal* and *Temora*, owed more to adaptation and free invention than translation. All were a great and controversial success. They were translated into German (by J. N. C. M. Denis) in 1768–9 and powerfully affected Herder and the German *Sturm und Drang*.

74 *The traveller will come*: this near-quotation anticipates the last fragment Werther will read aloud to Lotte. See page 103 and note.

75 *27 October, evening*: added in revision.

76 *I have lost . . . the holy, enlivening power*: compare this with Coleridge's 'Dejection: an Ode': 'I may not hope from outward forms to win | The passion and the life, whose fountains are within'; 'Ah! from the soul itself must issue forth | A light, a glory, a fair luminous cloud | Enveloping the earth …'.

   like a . . . broken pitcher: see Ecclesiastes 12: 6.

   when the sky above him is brass: see Deuteronomy 28: 23.

77 *Does not the Son of God Himself say*: alludes to John 6: 65.

   And if the chalice was too bitter: see Matthew 26: 39.

   My God, my God why hast thou forsaken me?: see Matthew 27: 46.

   Who rolls up the heavens like a cloth?: alludes to (or misquotes) Psalm 104: 2.

78 *22 November*: added in revision.

79 *26 November*: added in revision.

80 *States General*: till 1795 the name for the Netherlands.

81 *his unexpectedly returning son*: see the parable of the Prodigal Son, Luke 15: 11–24.

90 *there is no return*: here, as in the letter of 15 November, Werther echoes *Hamlet*, III. i. 56 ff.

93 *I write this to you*: writing this letter, Werther for the first time addresses Lotte in the familiar second-person singular form (*Du*).

96 *your translation of some of the poems of Ossian*: Goethe translated these poems in 1771, having been directed to Ossian by Herder. They are a sequence entitled 'The Songs of Selma'. He made a fair copy of his translation for Friederike Brion, and reworked it for *Werther*.

103 *Why wake me, airs of spring?*: this passage is taken not from 'The Songs of Selma' but from 'Berrathon', a quite separate poem. Goethe uses it here

because it resumes, in a different wording, the quotation on p. 74 and fits and exacerbates the situation Werther and Lotte are in.

105 *I go ahead, to my Father*: alludes to John 14: 28.

the following unsealed note: Werther's note is a less formal version of the one Jerusalem sent to Kestner asking to borrow his pistols.

110 *priest and the Levite . . . and the Samaritan*: see Luke 10: 31–3 and the Letter of 12 August.

the cold and fearful cup: see Matthew 26: 42, John 18: 11, and p. 77.

111 *Emilia Galotti*: a 'bürgerliches Trauerspiel' ('bourgeois tragedy') by Gotthold Ephraim Lessing (1729–81), first performed and published in 1772. A copy did indeed lie open on Jerusalem's desk. Emilia, virtuous and 'middle-class', gets her father to kill her, to save her from being debauched by the Prince. Lessing's play encouraged a more socially critical theatre, and for Werther, as for Jerusalem, it served as a pointer towards the social grounds of their suicides.

whom he had always loved best: perhaps alludes to John 13: 23.

MORE ABOUT **OXFORD WORLD'S CLASSICS**

The Oxford World's Classics Website

www.worldsclassics.co.uk

- Browse the full range of Oxford World's Classics online

- Sign up for our monthly e-alert to receive information on new titles

- Read extracts from the Introductions

- Listen to our editors and translators talk about the world's greatest literature with our Oxford World's Classics audio guides

- Join the conversation, follow us on Twitter at OWC_Oxford

- Teachers and lecturers can order inspection copies quickly and simply via our website

www.worldsclassics.co.uk

American Literature

British and Irish Literature

Children's Literature

Classics and Ancient Literature

Colonial Literature

Eastern Literature

European Literature

Gothic Literature

History

Medieval Literature

Oxford English Drama

Poetry

Philosophy

Politics

Religion

The Oxford Shakespeare

A complete list of Oxford World's Classics, including Authors in Context, Oxford English Drama, and the Oxford Shakespeare, is available in the UK from the Marketing Services Department, Oxford University Press, Great Clarendon Street, Oxford OX2 6DP, or visit the website at www.oup.com/uk/worldsclassics.

In the USA, visit www.oup.com/us/owc for a complete title list.

Oxford World's Classics are available from all good bookshops. In case of difficulty, customers in the UK should contact Oxford University Press Bookshop, 116 High Street, Oxford OX1 4BR.